DEDICATION

To all those who cherish their dreams.

THE MARKETPLACE

First Edition

Published by The Nazca Plains Corporation
Las Vegas, Nevada
2010

ISBN: 978-1-935509-89-9

Published by

The Nazca Plains Corporation ®
4640 Paradise Rd, Suite 141
Las Vegas NV 89109-8000

PUBLISHER'S NOTE
The Marketplace is a work of fiction created wholly by *Bill Smith*'s imagination. All characters are fictional and any resemblance to any persons living or deceased is purely by accident. No portion of this book reflects any real person or events.

Cover, Blake Stephens
Art Director, Blake Stephens

THE MARKETPLACE

First Edition

Bill Smith

CONTENTS

CHAPTER 1

"The Rio Experience"

I'd heard about the Brazilian markets since I was a kid and, undoubtedly, Rio's was the biggest with the highest quality, the greatest variety, uncomparable values, and, best of all, was the largest in the entire world. It was so big it had reached legendary proportions; it was so varied each category had to be divided into sections, then subsections, and then sub-subsections.

It was rumored that over a ton of slave chow was consumed by the stock on hand each day; that it took a permanent staff of 500 in-house slaves just to clean, feed, cage, and display the stock at the daily auctions for purchase; that the marketplace permanently employed over 50 metal smiths just to fit collars, rings, and restraints; that another 50 well-trained employees, called "enforcers," did nothing but mete out the punishments necessary to maintain the rigid slave discipline required in such a huge marketplace; that 10 employees did nothing but permanently mark new stock with glowing electric branding irons; that 15 veterinarians were on duty around the clock to trim the uncircumcised if that was a purchaser's desire or even castrate a hapless slave if he appeared unruly or if purchasers preferred eunuchs; and that it took five huge adjacent hotels just to house the thousands of buyers who visited the market each day.

Brochures recommended planning a minimum of four days just to browse prior to any serious buying; to allow at least two days for the purchasing experience itself allowing time for thorough examination, comparison shopping, and purchase negotiations; and another two days for body fittings, body modifications, and shipping preparations. In other words, allow at least eight days if you were a serious buyer.

Travel agents throughout the world promoted the "Rio Experience" and package tours were always available which combined your air arrangements, transfers to and from the airport, a good nearby hotel for your stay, a package of prepaid meals at some interesting restaurants, and a tour or two of the other sights Rio had to offer. Most package tours usually included some coupons for a night or two with a pleasure slave of your choosing from among the hotel's own disease-free, fresh, but well-trained stock; making arrangements for shipping purchased items back home (although the shipping charges themselves were on you); and, frequently, discount certificates for a 5 or even 10 percent markdown on purchased items at cooperating dealers. These deals were hard to beat in that the items purchased on your own usually cost considerably more and most visitors took advantage of the "package deals," even those not really interested in (or financially unable to) owning a slave themselves but who just enjoyed the ambience of a huge market in human flesh and the thrill of handling the beautiful compliant bodies up for sale on any given day.

At last, now almost 22 myself, I had the funds for the long anticipated trip to the Rio markets and, when I saw a really good deal at my local travel agent in Philadelphia, I bought a 10-day "Rio Experience" deluxe package complete with side trips to two famous night clubs, a tour of the Mardi Gras float preparation barns, an aerial tram to the top of the famed cross overlooking the city and five nights with my choice among the hotel's "pleasure service" staff. Best of all, on my 21st birthday, I had inherited the funds to buy a really high quality slave for my own personal use - possibly two, dependent on current prices.

CHAPTER 2

The Trip to Rio

The plane trip involved changing at Atlanta, but was otherwise uneventful. By the time I was through passport control, I spotted the little sign in the hands of my hotel's agent and soon was on my way to the luggage area where a hotel slave, a magnificent huge black man wearing only some tight Speedo-type shorts that revealed everything and a thick copper slave collar, gathered up my luggage effortlessly and took it to the awaiting van where two other passengers were already sitting in air-conditioned comfort sipping an iced cola furnished by the hotel agent from the van's ice box. The handsome black slave placed my luggage in the rear luggage compartment revealing his spectacular musculature in the process, and then, with a nod from the hotel agent, raced around to the driver's compartment to chauffeur us into the city itself.

"The boy's one of those available for your pleasure," the agent commented casually with a nod toward the porter/driver. "He's fully trained and guaranteed disease-free," he added as the 'boy' being discussed turned around and gave us a huge inviting smile.

"Well, he sure as hell knows how to suck," one of the fellow passengers commented. When I looked somewhat confused, he added, "Your plane was coming in just a few minutes after ours, so they asked us if we would mind waiting for you to save them a separate trip, offering...." he paused dramatically, "the use of this boy while we were waiting. All we had time for was a good sucking each, but the black's good, let me tell you, and it was unusually relaxing after such a long flight. I don't know about my partner here, but I was damn glad we had to wait a few minutes for you," he smiled.

His partner spoke for the first time. "I've got a couple of coupons for use of the hotel staff and I'm going to use one of them for a night with that black boy behind the wheel, believe you me. If he takes a fuck half as good as he sucks, it's going to be one hell of a night," he laughed. "That OK with you, black boy?" he asked the driver.

"Sure is, master," the black slave answered with another huge smile. "You won't be sorry you choose this black body for your enjoyment, master," he promised. "And I've got staying power, too, master. Good for the whole night, master!"

"The boy is talkative," the agent commented dryly. "But, by all reports, he is damn good in bed, no matter what you might want. Of course, there are many other choices available at the hotel. I wouldn't decide on anything until I'd looked all of them over - they're all well trained and eager to please if they know what's good for them. Of course, at the hotel they won't be covering themselves up like you see this boy here out in public."

I laughed to myself at the agent apologizing for the modesty of the black slave in his skin-tight tiny briefs that left absolutely nothing to the imagination in terms of his sexual apparatus. Obviously, we were a long way from the rather staid conventions of Philadelphia where slaves outside their owner's homes usually had most of their bodies covered and clothing was generally loose fitting and unrevealing at best. In fact, the Quaker City seemed to dress slaves so they appeared to be sexless automatons who only uttered an occasional "Yes, mistress," or "Right away, master," to demonstrate they were still human. But, of course, inside the privacy of an owner's home, slaves could be shown any way their master desired, and some owners, those primarily possessing slaves as sex objects, often kept their properties butt naked at all times so they could enjoy the sight. But here in Rio, the differences between public and private display of slaves seem considerably more diluted if the black chauffeur was any example.

The trip into town confirmed I was now in a more flamboyant culture. Most slaves were scantily dressed in the tropical climate if at all. Indeed, it seemed a good number of slaves were kept nude at all times, no matter where they were at judging from the lack of tan lines on their bodies. And it quickly became apparent that the better the slave's body, the less likely he would be clothed. The only slaves that had on full body clothing, like a tunic or a shirt and trousers, were those old or ugly or those disfigured from over zealous trainers somewhere alone the line. Those young, well built, handsome and with decent sexual equipment were invariably kept in the buff where everyone could enjoy their bodies. The tight Speedos on our black chauffeur was quite modest compared to what we saw on the streets outside our van windows.

The agent noticed me staring at all the naked slaves out on the streets. "It's warm enough here we don't really need clothes, so why waste the costs of clothes and all the laundry that goes with it in this heat?"

The answer was self-evident so I just nodded my understanding.

"Of course, most of these slaves are just trash compared to what you'll be seeing at the market. Even the maintenance staff at the hotel puts most of these street slaves to shame."

"Well, if the driver is any example of the hotel's staff, I can't imagine much better at the market," I addressed the agent.

"Him?" he snorted. "That's a B-grade slave. The A-grades for sale at the market are so much better than him there's no comparison. Wait until you look an A-grade slave over thoroughly. You'll see the differences loud and clear."

"Like what?" I challenged, looking again at the magnificent musculature and the handsome face of the slave driving the van.

"I've been here before," one of the fellow passengers interjected, "and the agent is absolutely correct. There's big differences between a B-grade and A-grade slave. The price differentiation between an A and a B is not just some hyped-up pricing gimmick. First of all, A-grades are all between 18 and 25, have almost perfect musculature on big well-boned physiques, are exceptionally handsome

- strikingly so - usually with some unusually attractive features such as long eye lashes, deep bright eyes, a spectacularly smooth complexion, long swan-like necks or thick, extremely muscular necks, thin waists relative to their heavy musculature, flowing light blond or red hair, high cheek bones, and abs resembling six-packs. They almost always have large suckable tits atop beautifully sculpted pectorals. An A-grade generally is bubble-butted with thick, well shaped thighs and invariably has an unusually long very thick circumcised prick of perfect proportions atop two well shaped large balls that protrude outward for maximum display without the need of genital rings or other forced protrusion devices. A-grades are very easy to arouse sexually and are noted for prodigious output. Their training allows them to perform on demand without hesitation, repeatedly if desired, with either sex and without any shame or humiliation evident. B-grades can do all of that, of course, but they just don't do it quite as well - there are little imperfections in their bodies, their sexual equipment is just a little less monumental, or their training doesn't quite hide some lingering humiliation or shame in being sexually used. Nothing wrong with a B-grade - especially when you take the price factors into account - they're often a great buy - but they're clearly not A-grade material and never will be, no matter how much good solid whip training they've had over the years. That black driving the van is a good example of a B-grade. He's got a great body with a well developed musculature, but his waist is a little too thick, his pecs could be just a little more puffed out, his cheekbones could be more pronounced, and his black eyes, although quite handsome on him, aren't the striking greens and blues and golds you often see in the A-grades. I haven't seen him stripped down yet, but, judging from what I can see through those Speedos he's wearing, he apparently needs the genital ring he's fitted with to show his equipment off really well and his prick looks to only be about 8 to 9 inches soft, although it certainly appears to be mighty thick. An A-grade slave has a prick about as big soft as hard - usually a good 10 to 13 inches long - really exceptional - and proportionally thick. Me, I always look for B-grade slaves. They're a much better value and they're just as good in bed any day if you ask me. I think A-grades are sold to those who only are satisfied with the highest priced slaves on the market or those who are buying them primarily for display. In bed, you can't tell a peso's difference between a well trained B-grade and an A-grade slave. For example, I challenge you to find an A-grade slave that sucks better than that black driver up there!"

"Is there a C-grade slave?" I innocently asked.

"Damn right there are, along with D-grades and E-grades, clear down to H-grades which are as close to walking dog food as you can get. In fact, that's who buys H-grade slaves - dog food and fertilizer producers. Even the medical research firms buy up G-grade slaves just so the research is valid. This human garbage you see on the streets out there is mainly C through F-grade slaves - ordinary looking slaves not so young anymore who still have a lot of work left in them. They may even be well hung, but their overall appearance mitigates against their use sexually. Hell, most all the male slaves are sterilized so they can't breed. That's closely managed anymore so the breed is improved rather than left up to chance, but you'll notice a good number of the women slaves are pregnant - put to the proper stud they can at least produce the next generation of slaves, but probably a good level upgrade in the process of selectively breeding them. Just good animal husbandry - you can get 10 to 15 new slaves out of a carefully bred bitch put to a good stud on a proper schedule."

I glanced out the van's windows again and did find most of the women slaves, easily identified by their collars and lack of clothing, were in some stage of visible pregnancy. As my fellow passenger had pointed out, most of the slaves were not particularly beautiful or handsome, most were not of exceptional physique, although their heavy work kept their muscles in good shape, and most were unexceptional in their sexual apparatus. Nothing wrong with them particularly - they were strong, well muscled and all looked healthy and disease free - but they weren't exceptional in any discernible way. When I really studied them, they seemed to be hard working without undue motivation from their whip-wielding overseers, obedient to their overseers' commands without hesitation or resistance, and with a look of acceptance of their status clearly evident. They gave the impression they accepted their slavery, knew they would never be anything but a slave, and were content they were healthy, well fed, and given shelter when needed. They were collared possessions and clearly understood their place in the world.

CHAPTER 3

The Rio Hotel

As I observed and speculated, we drew up to the off-street private entrance of the hotel whereupon all pretense of slave modesty collapsed. Instantly, the luggage was unloaded by a corps of handsome nude porters while butt naked bell boys took each of us to our reserved rooms. Enroute, each of us was given a tour of the hotel's 'pleasure staff' on full display in a side room off the main lobby. There we saw about 10 female and 10 male slaves each on a separate pedestal, posing and preening like classic statues, each thrusting their genitals out in a most inviting fashion while seductive smiles issued from each and every one. Below each pedestal was a number.

"If you see any you want right now, just point and we'll have them up in your suite within five minutes. If you see one you'd like later on, just tell me the number and I'll reserve it for your use whenever you want. But, if you want to wait until later to choose, they'll still be on display for you to pick - unless someone else is using them right then - but, if so, another one just as good will be up on display," the bellhop announced as we slowed down for a good look.

"I want that black van driver," one of my fellows told the bellhop. "Soon as you can get him up to my room."

"Yes, master," the bellhop answered with a smile. "It'll take about 15 minutes to get him ready for you - we'll clean him out inside and out, then oil his body, and lube his hole. No more than 15 minutes max, master," the bellhop promised.

"I'll take #6," my other fellow announced. I quickly turned to look at his choice standing there on the display pedestal. The slave was a young female, no more than 19 or so, with long black hair, a flawless olive complexion, beautiful full tits, and a nicely shaped body. Her body was shaved clean below her eyelashes so her sex was fully displayed. "Had her last month when I was here," he muttered.

"Yes, master," the bellhop replied. "She can go up with us now if you want in that she's fully prepared for usage, or I can give you time to get settled if you prefer."

"Take her with us," the client muttered, "if her's hole well lubed. I enjoy fucking them on both sides."

"Of course, master," the bellhop replied, seeing nothing unusual in the request - not too surprising since he had been vigorously butt fucked by a hotel client less than an hour before and had cleaned himself out only minutes before the van had arrived.

"Anyone for you, master?" the bellhop asked me cheerfully.

"Don't think so. I'll save my coupons for later," I replied, whereupon he took me immediately to my suite. Once there, he adjusted the thermostat, checked the bathroom, and hung my light jacket up in the closet. It gave me a chance to study him. He was about 6 feet tall, beautifully muscled, had a creamy light ivory complexion with reddish blond hair, Grecian type facial features with an absolutely straight nose and high cheekbones, and his fully shaved body featured some nicely protruding pecs with large ringed nipples as well as a long and thick penis, partially erect, thrust into protrusion due to a wide genital band welded around both balls and the base of his thick prick. He was, in total, a beautiful specimen of a mature man.

The bellboy saw me looking at him as if I was evaluating a horse up for auction and blushed becomingly, thrusting his pelvis out slightly to better display himself without appearing obvious.

"Are you cleaned out and lubed?" I asked forthrightly, surprised I could be so open here in Brazil, considering my staid Philadelphia background.

"Yes, master," the white slave whispered, blushing bright red in the process, his eyes cast to the floor.

"Can I use a coupon on you?" I asked, referring to the hotel's promotion where guests had access to sexual use of at least certain of their staff.

"Yes, master," the red head answered, blushing even a deeper shade of red. "Would you like to use me now, master?"

"Why not?" I responded. "I can always buy some extra coupons later, I suppose."

"Yes, master. You can buy additional coupons very cheaply if you're a guest and they are simply added to your bill. I can get them for you when you are through using me if you want, master."

"Fine. On your knees in front of me, boy. We can start with a good sucking and then I think I'll fuck you with you leaning over the arm of this chair. That's just the right height for me and I can get it all the way in you that way."

"Yes, master," the slave said as he quickly settled down on his knees, opened his mouth wide, and, as soon as I had my pants and undershorts off, swallowed me all the way down and began churning his tongue around the length of my shaft while sucking vigorously.

I was surprised how good he was at this and wondered how much training it takes to produce a slave with such skill in this area. The slave's eyes were trained on my face to judge my reactions to his efforts so it was obvious he was crying silently as he faultlessly complied with this latest hotel guest's wishes. I was so carried away with his efforts I wasn't in the mood to find out why he would be crying or really didn't even care at that point. It was all I could do to keep from shooting off in his mouth before I ordered him over the arm of the chair with legs spread wide so his hole was fully open and conveniently accessible. Just like he said, he was generously lubed in preparation for just this type of usage and I inserted my full erection all the way in him easily and then pumped away with abandon, ignoring his little whimpers and groans until I had deposited a full load of hot cum deep inside him.

As soon as I was spent and pulled out, the slave immediately turned around and cleaned my prick with his tongue of the cum, ass juices, and lube still clinging to it, swallowing everything neatly away with the obligatory "Thank you, master, for using me," uttered softly as he again bowed his head before me awaiting further commands.

"Have you been a slave all your life?" I asked, pondering just why he had been crying when he was servicing me.

"No master," the slave responded. "I was enslaved just six months ago and only finished training a couple of weeks ago, master."

"You're training seems incomplete, slave. You suck well and you take to a good fucking well too, but you don't see a well trained slave crying when he's chosen for use and all that blushing when I was looking you over made you look like a slave brand new to an owner's demands. Most disconcerting. I'll speak to the hotel manager about it when I get a chance."

The slave froze in obvious fear and I could see him biting his lip in panic. He didn't dare to comment on my intended action, of course, but he couldn't help a fresh round of tears spilling down his cheeks as he knew the horrible punishments awaiting any slave that received any comments even remotely negative about a hotel slave from one of the guests.

"And until six months ago, just what were you up to, slave?" I asked.

The red head quickly regained control. "I was an apprentice mason in Belfast, Ireland, master, close to getting my master's license. I got drunk one night at the local pub and drove my trunk right into a passenger car, killing a 8-year-old girl and injuring both of her parents badly. The courts sentenced me to lifetime slavery with the proviso I be sold to a slave exporter so the girl's family would never have to look at me again. I was sold in a wholesale lot to a Brazilian slave importer located right her in Rio and when my basic slave training was completed, I was sold at auction to the hotel here, master."

"Why the blushing and crying if you had the standard slave training?" I asked.

"I was particularly naive about slavery and what they do, master. In Belfast, the only slaves I met were all construction workers like myself more or less - they were all clothed and housed in separate dorms at night - and the only difference I ever saw was that they were collared and faced a whipping if they didn't meet their production quotas every day so they were hard workers who didn't goof around. I knew their sex life was limited to studding the women slaves when that's what their owner wanted and fooling around with each other when that wasn't enough, but I never knew it went much beyond that so I didn't ever ask them about it one way or the other. I almost envied them in that they didn't have to pay any taxes, worry about unemployment, or wonder if their pay check would buy enough food to last until their next pay check like me and the other free guys had to. Besides, their owners had to pay for medical care when they got sick, provide all their shelter and food, and keep them up proper so they would retain their value if they had to be sold - all things I had to worry about for myself. Shall I continue, master, or am I talking too much?"

"Continue, slave," I commanded.

"Once I was in slave training down here, it was made clear our new owners would probably have us go around naked most of the time, would expect us to be fully available for any and all sexual duties at any time by anybody, and we were not only going to do this properly, but were going to flaunt our bodies' availability at every opportunity to both free men and free women as well as perform sexually with other slaves when our new owners desired that as a form of entertainment. It takes a bit of getting used to, master, for a Catholic boy brought up in the old ways not used to slavery much. It still shows, master, when I start blushing and crying sometimes but I'm getting a lot better, master, at controlling myself. Just two weeks ago, I was crying openly and blushed clear down to my toes, master, but now, I can tell I'm adjusting and won't be bringing all those well deserved beatings on myself so often. I'm sincerely sorry if I offended you, master, and I know it embarrasses the hotel. I'm working on correcting myself as fast as I can, master."

"Well, adjust or get beaten to death. It's your choice, isn't it, slave?" I commented coldly.

"Yes, master. They told me yesterday if I don't shape up, they're going to sell me off to the emerald mines," the slave blurted out with obvious terror.

"So, what's so bad about that, slave?"

"Master, a slave sent to the mines never sees daylight again and usually lasts less than a year under the whips there. Better to be beaten to death here in Rio, master."

"Well, stop all that silly blushing and tearing up, slave. That's simple enough. It's not like there's anything to be embarrassed about. After all, you're just a slave and people have every right to look you over naked and paw over your sexual parts - they own you, after all. And getting screwed or having to swallow a big one isn't anything to get emotional about - it's not like it was wrong or anything for a slave. Just the opposite, actually. That's what slaves are for. An owner would be crazy not to take advantage of the pleasure a good looking slave's body can give him, wouldn't he? If you were lucky enough to own a decent looking slave boy, wouldn't you have him suck you off every chance you got or plow his rear end if you needed some relief?"

The slave brightened, looked up, and promptly retorted, "Yes, master."

"Well, see there. It's only natural slaves are going to be looked over, fucked, and told to give a good suck. It's just part of slavery. It has nothing to do with the slaves or the masters - it's just the natural order of things when you have slaves in a society. I'm surprised you can't understand that. After all, they've had slaves in Ireland since time immemorial. I suppose you were so poor you never were around them much so, obviously, you'd never thought it out."

"No, master, but it certainly makes sense, master."

"Of course it does, slave. When you get your beating tonight, think it over and I predict, once you understand it, your problems of blushing and crying are all behind you. A good slave takes pride in the pleasures his body can offer his master."

"Yes, master. I'm sure I'll do better now and I thank you for your taking the time to help this slave, master. It's much appreciated, master. The only way I know how to repay you properly, master, is to offer you use of my body again, and this time, master, I guarantee you I won't ruin it with any silly blushing or trembling or crying, master," the slave promised as he thrust his banded sexual apparatus out invitingly.

I took the slave up on his invitation since I was feeling a little rejuvenated by now and the slave was good for his word this time around. He offered his body up freely without any signs of reservation or emotional reaction, used every technique he knew of to enhance my pleasure in using him, and, as proof of his new attitude, when I was fucking him, he struggled to keep from shooting off himself until finally I granted my permission when I dumped into his hole once again and felt him shudder as load after load of thick hot cum pumped out of his prick onto the arm of the sofa beneath him. As he screamed ecstatically in the throes of orgasm, I knew his problems of adjustment were behind him. As I patted his ass in dismissal, he turned around and gave me a huge smile.

"Thank you, master, for helping me," he said with such sincerity I knew he too was aware his blushing and crying problems were history now. They had been replaced with the far healthier attitude of enjoying what he was doing to the fullest and letting his body respond accordingly. His value to the hotel just shot up a good 100% and one slave headed toward the emerald mines was now aimed toward a happy, fulfilling life as a naked hotel bellhop.

When I went to give him the coupon, he took it, but said the next use was "on him" any time I wanted it as long as the hotel management would allow him the time and he would view it as "an honor" to be fucked by anyone as smart as I was. I assured him I would "honor" him every chance I got on my stay in Rio. When I motioned I was through with him, he bowed and thanked me again for using him and promptly left, no doubt to report back to the hotel management as to his whereabouts and to turn in the coupon.

I debated whether to report him to management for his crying behavior or not in view of the free usage he offered me, but decided slave discipline had to be consistent and his offer to let me use his body free could be seen as a bribe, so I called the front desk and reported the incident, indicating I didn't think they had to worry about it ever happening again. They thanked me and said the slave would receive 10 lashes of the cane before being caged for the night as an "encouragement" of the Irish slave's efforts to improve himself. They also said an extra coupon for use of a pleasure slave of my choice would be the hotel's way of thanking me for reporting the slave and that I could pick it up the next time I passed the front desk.

Breakfast the next morning was buffet style, but the waiters on hand for coffee and to help carry your plates were obviously expensive and probably the best the nearby slave markets could provide. Each was completely nude, of course, to best display their bodies and their musculature, definition and overall beauty were just stunning. Other than the carefully coiffured hair on their head, their bodies were absolutely hairless, giving a look of absolute cleanliness (appropriate for food servers), youthfulness, availability, and, best of all, displayed their sexual equipment unabashedly. This morning, 'Eggs Rio Esclavo' were being featured: two poached eggs served on a toasted English muffin and topped with a thick hot cum sauce, pumped fresh from a small squad of 'milk slaves' on duty that morning, one of which was assigned to your table when the dish was delivered to make sure it was as hot and fresh as possible. When I placed my order for the specialty, the head waiter asked me to pick out the 'saucer' I would prefer from those standing on display nearby. I picked out the black who chauffeured us in from the airport yesterday. He recognized me and smiled brightly as I pointed to him. Now totally nude, of course, it was obvious the tight Speedo he was in yesterday only hinted at what was available. He was about the best hung black I had ever seen, and judging from his huge dripping erection, his duties last night in satisfying one of my fellow passengers had not dampened his ardor in any way.

When the 'Eggs Rio Esclavo' arrived, the 'esclavo' part of the formula had his monstrous prick swaying directly over the breakfast dish waiting to provide the hot sauce topping. First, I tried to encompass his huge balls in my right hand as he stood perfectly still (but shuddered slightly) as I squeezed the swollen ball sac hard. Then I wrapped my left hand as far as it would go around the thick shaft and started pumping it vigorously. He instantly got rock hard and, after less than 12 strokes, was shooting a load of steaming, thick cum atop the poached eggs, completely covering them in the process as the source of the sauce broke out into a full body sweat and momentarily panted and bucked just a little as he emptied his balls (which quickly felt soft and spongy after he had completely emptied). I patted him on his rump in dismissal when the last drop was extracted and the black, still partially erect and smiling, retreated quietly back to the group of 'saucers' and again assumed a full display position.

Many other hotel guests were breakfasting, most choosing the 'Eggs Rio Esclavo' special which kept the available 'saucer' slaves busy. At one point, all were emptying their balls at customer's tables and yet another order was ready. No problem! Immediately one of the coffee servers filled in, then yet another, and finally, as the volume of orders keep flowing in, even the head waiter had his prick over the dish as yet another customer pumped a load out of him. The smell of all that fresh cum, mixed with the rich aroma of the Brazilian coffees and the fragrance of sex sweat off of the freshly washed bodies of the hotel's choice slaves gave the restaurant a distinctive Rio air: exotic, sensual, and indulging.

I looked around for my two companions from the transit van yesterday but didn't spot either one: they were probably still sound asleep after a satisfying engagement with the hotel's 'coupon' slaves. Sopping up the last of the hot cum with the remnants of the English muffin while enjoying a second cup of the embracing black coffee, I planned the day's activities.

CHAPTER 4

Learning About The Marketplace

Knowing I couldn't see everything of the market that I desired in a single day - or even five days - I decided to try to get a general overview the first day, spend the entire second day perusing the market for the highly trained work slaves I had heard so much about, use the third day to try to find myself a black sex slave worth shipping home, and use the fourth day to look over some white slaves since I was considering buying a white if one really turned me on, was well trained, and affordable. I wasn't too worried, though. Whatever I bought and shipped home, I felt I could easily sell them at considerable profit in the Philadelphia markets where slaves were, overall, considerably more expensive, not having access to the output of the numerous breeding farms that surrounded Rio and which operated at full capacity year after year for the huge Rio market which was open 365 days a year. At night, I planned to explore more of the hotel's coupon offerings, take in the two notorious nightclubs built into

my tour, and, if all went well, start sampling some of the
goods I had bought locally. Somehow, in between all this,
I hoped to take in some of the famous sight-seeing spots
other than the biggest tourist draw - the huge slave market.
The remainder of the days I would leave unplanned at
this point, waiting to see what turned up.

I drained the last of the coffee from my cup, watched
as the black chauffeur was once again spurting out a fresh
load for another order of 'Eggs Rio Esclavo' at a nearby
table (marveling at his stamina in this assignment), and,
with directions from the front desk, started out to the
marketplace, the main entrance of which was just two
blocks away. While at the front desk, I inquired as to how
much a slave like the black who was driving the airport
transit yesterday and who was now serving as a milk stud
in the dining room cost currently.

"Oh, you mean 'Handy'," he smiled, pointing to
him in a group picture of the entire hotel slave staff in back
of the desk to make sure he had identified him correctly.

"Yes," I said.

"Slaves like him run from $200,000 to $250,000
generally - top quality. You can find them under the 'Select
Sex Slaves' areas at the marketplace in the area devoted to
blacks. But, if you want, we can give you a sales quote on
him. It will run within that price range although he has,
of course, been heavily used here at the hotel. But we feel
that's offset by the fact he's proven his worth and buyers
can see for themselves his training is superb."

"I could buy him from the hotel at about the same
price I would pay at the market?" I asked.

"That's right, sir. He's hardly a virgin, but he's a proven well-trained whore," the clerk said with a chuckle. "At this point, he's about as far away from a virgin as you can get," he laughed, "but damn few slaves can pump out a nice big load three times in one morning for our breakfast special. Did you have the 'Rio Eggs Esclavo' this morning, sir?"

"Yes, and that black boy sauced it for me," I chuckled back, "even though my friend had him in his bed all last night so I doubt if the slave got much rest."

"Well, there you have it, then, sir. Nothing like a well trained whore boy when it comes to delivering the goods. Think about it when you're looking over the fresh stock at the marketplace. They'll have some alleged virgins up on the block with tight little assholes and unstretched throats, but will they have the proven stamina, the performance only a lot of experience can provide, and positive attitude you see in the hotel's staff?"

"You're quite a salesman," I laughed. "I didn't even know the hotel sold off their staff on request."

"Yes, sir. We like a bit of turnover. Keeps the stock fresh and there's always something new for frequent guests that way."

"I imagine you wear a slave out pretty fast around here what with this coupon business," I added drily.

"I have to agree with you there, sir. If a guest doesn't buy them from us after two or three years of duty here, we usually take them down the street to the market and trade them in on fresh stock."

'How do you know they're fresh?" I inquired, eager to pick up some tricks of the trade.

"Well, it's easy, sir. First, you look at stock just shipped in from the breeding farms - they're fresh except for the heavy training they've had. That black boy you were asking about is an example of that source, sir. Or you can stick with newly enslaved stock - no more than six months since their enslavement, mind you - so they've had time to get through a complete training regimen but haven't been fucked to death yet. That bell boy you had last night is a good example of that venue, sir. And with either source, you can tell when you look them over - they should have a good tight ass but trained enough to allow your fingers easy entry all the way in and you should be able to stick your fingers all the way down their throats without having them gag on you. That's the sign of a well-trained slave. And they should still shudder a bit when you poke your fingers up them or squeeze their tits or heft up their balls. It takes more than six months training to get rid of those tell-tale traits of a near virgin. Just to make sure, sir, it's always wise to ask for a personal inspection and, once you're in the privacy booth, see for yourself how they take your prick down their throat or all the way up their ass. The pretty well used stock just takes all that in stride without much reaction one way or the other, although they'll fake these little squeals and moans as if it's their first time, but you can always tell. The fresh stock gasps and tremors no matter how hard they try to hide it. Some, no matter how hard they try - knowing they'll get a beating for it - break out crying or sobbing, like that Irish slave you had yesterday afternoon. They'll get over that quick enough with regular use, but it's a sure sign of stock that's still nice and fresh."

"Thanks for the tips," I said as I turned and left, my prick already hard and dripping just thinking about my shopping expedition.

CHAPTER 5

My First Impressions of The Marketplace

The entrance to the marketplace was spectacular. Each specialized section displayed an example of what they had to offer on podiums lining the main entry.

One side was devoted to female slaves arranged chronologically: 18 to 25-year-olds (the beautiful marketed as bed slaves, household maids, and secretarial help and breeding stock while they were performing their other duties); the non-beautiful marketed as factory workers, cooks, gardeners, janitors, launderers, miners, plantation field workers and, again, breeding stock in addition to their other duties); middle-aged women for more advanced positions requiring considerable training and skill (supervisors, administrators, planners, purchasing agents, overseers, etc); and older women (for nannies, nursing attendants, and inventory control). The greatest space was taken up by the girls being sold for sexual usage as one would expect and it was clear that's where the greatest number of women slaves were being trained and marketed.

Only the ugly were marketed to mines, plantations, sanitation departments, and manufacturing assembly line work where a sturdy, muscular body no more than 30 years old could be purchased for little more than the price of a good used car. The ads accompanying these 'industrial' slaves pointed out the financial advantages: 20 to 30 good years of work 16-hours-a-day, 7 days-a-week, 365 days-a-year for little more than the cost of their feed, stabling them, and the costs of keeping them well motivated with the whip or other devices. As they pointed out, it was cheaper than any automated robot, any free labor no matter what the pay, and usually considerably cheaper than the diesel fuel or electricity needed to power labor-saving machinery.

"Why save labor when labor is practically free?" the signs proclaimed and the point was well taken in a slave economy. As a result, almost all trucks, TVs, and other household and industrial needs were now produced with slave power, practically solving the world's industrial pollution problems in one easy stroke.

The advertisements did get me thinking. I produced components for cell phones at a small assembly plant right in Philadelphia that took about 70 employees currently to keep up with demand. They worked (at best) 40 hours a week. My contribution to the employees' health insurance was running $17,500 a month, the 401(K) contributions were another $20,000 a month, and I still was paying them around $16.80 an hour on the average. Slaves could be worked 112 hours a week; the feed would run around $4 a day, caging them at night would cost around $6 a week, and I'd have to have one slave overseer for every 10 workers to maintain full productivity 16 hours-a-day so, for 70 workers, I'd need to buy 77 slaves. [Slave overseers worked out fine in practice because their privileged position was taken away immediately and they were transferred to the work force if they failed to extract the last ounce of energy out of the slaves under their charge without damaging the property.] The sex of the slave wouldn't make much difference in this line of work, although female slaves would have the advantage of producing a whole new crop of slave pups each and every year while they were working away. The new crop would probably be about as ugly as their mothers despite how handsome the studs were I put them to, but they could be raised and sold off as industrial workers for a handsome additional long-term profit. If I could buy up some of these industrial slaves still in their early 20s or even their late teens for $10,000 to $15,000 apiece, I could price my assembled components lower than any competitor and still assure myself some huge profits. The downside was the slaves could always get sick and die on you, they wore out after 20 or 30 years and had to be replaced, and maintenance costs might go up with inflation, but, in the interim, they would probably hold their resale value for a good 10 or 20 years at least and, if the whole thing didn't work out, you could always sell the lot of them off in Philadelphia markets at a considerable profit and go back to hiring in free labor.

Looking around, I made up my mind: I would buy 70 female industrial slaves no older than 22 or so, pick them for their sturdiness and general health overlooking their looks (actually the uglier, the better the buyer's price); make sure they were fertile so they could be easily bred on a regular basis; and buy 7 male 'overseer' industrial slaves who were as big as they come, hung like horses, and as good looking as I could find in this cheap category in that I planned to use them as studs as well as overseers for their assigned work groups - sort of a tyrannical husband with ten hard working wives would make up a "work team" at my factory. The husband held the whip and kept them pregnant; the wives worked day and night to avoid the harshest punishments from the every present whip and were resigned to being fucked steadily whenever they weren't pregnant until they were once again. Females would be a better choice if they already bore the tell-tale stretch lines of previous pregnancies indicating they were proven breeders and the males would be a better choice if they had sired some offspring to date and who were the type that took pride in meeting production goals no matter what it took to reach them, tempered with great respect for the value of his owner's property.

Once that decision was made, I knew I didn't need to buy them today, but would wait until closer to the time I was going home eight or nine days down the road - it would save on holding cage costs and perhaps I could arrange buying them as a lot with a big discount involved.

On the other side of the marketplace entry were examples of each of the categories of male slaves offered. Despite the fact one male could stud 500 females for breeding purposes, male slaves were just as popular as females in the Brazilian markets and they actually cost considerably more. This was because they were more versatile: male slaves were usually stronger and could do tasks requiring huge amounts of raw muscular strength; males had often received more formalized training before being enslaved and some possessed highly specialized skills requiring considerable training; male slaves retained their value longer, so they made a better investment in the long haul; male slaves could be used sexually by male owners without any complications of unwanted babies or the romantic charades often concocted by male slave's mistresses; and males could take more heavy discipline without breaking down in the process. On the downside, male slaves ate more, had greater health problems and didn't live as long, didn't have the endurance of women slaves, had debilitating orgasms if being used by women owners who wanted their services longer than they were capable sometimes, and some were often difficult to control due to their excessive aggression (although this was usually easily cured by a quick and easily arranged castration). Surprisingly, though, male slaves were more loyal to their masters or mistresses once they were properly broken than female slaves who tended to have more well-hidden concern about themselves and their slave brethren than their owners' welfare.

Consequently, male slaves were divided into many more categories of specialization and types. Like the women slave offerings, they were first arranged into two main categories: 18 to 25 year-olds and mature adult stock. Within each division, there were basic subdivisions by color, ethnic origins, languages understood, physique size, musculature, masculine body attributes, training to date, overall attractiveness, age, specialized training, and age.

Work and draft slaves were the biggest categories, of course, with black draft slaves being the most numerous and the cheapest. Most of this category were notable for huge musculatures, big sturdy physiques, high disease resistance, illiteracy with poor speaking abilities, sex organs almost always semi-erect and dripping due to chronic unfulfilled need, and bodies permanently scarred by numerous whip welts, hot iron brands, and electric prods as they had been broken, trained, and then kept motivated to their assigned tasks. Although all were collared with heavy iron bands welded tight around their throats, little money was wasted on other decorations other than many had their ankles permanently shackled to limit mobility to anything but a 18" shuffle. Some buyers would nose ring them; a few others would ring their tits; still others would band their genitals or clip their ears - but such control devices really weren't necessary once they'd been broken and they really weren't worth decorating.

But to show what could be done with a little imagination, one display showed a matched team of palanquin bearers up for sale hitched to a typical palanquin as part of the demonstration: all were the same height, weight, and musculature; all were dark brown 3/4 African, 1/4 Latino mixtures; all were equally well hung; all were completely body shaved save their long black head hair braided into dread-locks; and all were fitted with fancy engraved bronze collars; matching genital bands insuring full protrusion of their large well-shaped circumcised genitals; all had huge bronze ear rings permanently dangling down to their shoulders; all had a matching nose ring fastened through the nose septum and then welded shut; and all sported large heavy bronze tit rings atop each heavily muscled pec. Holding the heavy palanquin aloft on their muscular shoulders with chains attaching their collars to the shafts of the palanquin, the slave bearers were magnificent in display: their bodies steaming with the sweat of their exertion; a visage of total control as they stood with legs wide apart to show off their beautifully ringed genitals, their postures ramrod straight, and their short leashes taut connecting their neck collars to the palanquin itself. They were offered as a team of four only but the price was surprisingly low in my opinion: the team of four completely fitted out were priced at about what five regular draft slaves of the same age and build would cost. I could see, at this price, why you saw so many Brazilians riding around the streets of Rio in the comfortable conveyance. The total costs of a showy palanquin, a team of even more showy slave bearers, and a stable to keep them in costs no more than an Italian motor scooter and, with a good whip, wasn't too much slower in getting around town.

Down toward the end of the long line of sample goods (designed as a guide for the new shopper), the slaves' appearance suddenly got much better. It was the area demonstrating the wares to be had in the male sex slave section. They had examples of each subsection: black, brown, tan, olive, white, yellow, and cream colors were all available. These came with black, brown, blond, red, white, and gray hair along with black, brown, gray, green, blue, and even golden hue eyes. There were hirsute as well as totally hairless bodies; heavily muscled, weightlifter bodies; swimmers bodies; well proportioned bodies next to the thin model-type bodies with tiny waists; and even fem bodies. There were bodies with full head hair in a variety of styles; bodies with well trimmed beards of various types; and bodies decorated with colorful tattoos and unique brands. There were men with gigantic thick, long penises; men with very thick, but short penises; men with long thin penises; men circumcised and men uncut; men with huge up-close balls and men with balls handing very low on their bodies, men who seemed to be in a perpetual state of erection and those who stood there flaccid; men with their balls cut off in a partial castration; and men with a full castration where only a scar and a small hole to piss out of remained. There were men with round 'bubble butts' riding high on their body; men with butts that looked like a mass of muscle; men with open holes that 'winked' at you; men with fat asses that looked like women's butts.

But all had one thing in common. They were extremely good looking sex objects to be used at a buyer's discretion, and providing pleasure was their purpose in life now. By the look on their handsome faces as they stood there in full naked display, most realized their new destiny and most accepted it, understanding they really had no alternatives. And, indeed, compared to the fate of a slave destined for the mines or construction work, they had lucked out! As long as their body could please a new owner to his complete satisfaction, they lives would be secure and, relative to other slaves, luxurious. Their open pleas to buy them reflected the fact they knew just how lucky they were no matter what was going to be demanded of them in some owner's bed or in demonstration at some new master's party. Whatever it was, it couldn't be anything more difficult than what had been demanded of them in the rigorous and demanding training sessions they had just completed.

Just looking these few absolutely breathtakingly beautiful specimens over, I wondered whether my hots for the black slave driving the van yesterday was a little premature, even though his huge prick and the loads that came out of it so easily were appealing. Compared to what I saw here, he wasn't all that special - competitive, but not outstanding, just as the hotel clerk had indicated when talking about his selling price. The desk clerk had given sound advice when he suggested looking around before deciding anything. As I looked around some more at just these examples of what was available in the full market, I even began to wonder if I really was dead set on having a black bed buck for my pleasure. Here there were some unbelievably good looking light skinned Latinos; some real blond beauties from the Slavic countries; some striking Arabs from the Middle East; some Mediterranean/Italian types that were so sexy I got hard just looking at them;

and some Indonesian boys that looked totally innocent and totally wanton at the same time. There was even a Canadian pure white on display that you just wanted to fuck then and there.

Without hesitation, I ignored my intent to look at all the market had to offer and headed straight for the subsection specializing in male sex slaves. Just shows what raging hormones will do, I chuckled to myself, as I followed the signs to the male sex slave sections. En route I bypassed signs pointing to transportation slaves, mining slaves, farm slaves, general laborers, gardening slaves, household servants, chefs, musicians, dancers, accountants, maintenance workers, factory slaves, mi'lady's studs, garage workers, warehouse slaves, dock slaves; merchandising (sales) slaves, restaurant slaves, hotel workers, overseer slaves, and on and on in hundreds of more categories. There were even signs pointing to "clearance sale," "going out of business sale," "estate sales," and "consignment shop."

But the one that slowed me down a little in my excitement was "bred to order pickups" and "breeder's errors outlet." I later found out this latter category sold birth defects and mutations that were considered marketable for one reason or another and the pregnancy had been allowed to continue after the first sonograms - most slaves produced on the breeding farms that fell into this unfortunate category were aborted long before birth of course. I also found out later that the "bred to order pickup" was just what it said it was: you ordered a slave to your exact specifications. The breeders arranged the proper stud and brood to produce such an order; training was arranged once the slave pup was born to enhance the genetic base, and approximately 18 years later, you picked up the finished product - obviously this was for long-range planners.

CHAPTER 6

Mi'Lady's Stud Boutique and Meeting Ramon

The very first area of the huge male sex slave section was the "mi'lady's studs boutique" and my curiosity got the best of me. The area, beautifully decorated and luxuriously furnished, was, as you would expect, populated primarily by hordes of eager women buyers. But some men, probably curious and nosy like myself were evident here and there among the obviously wealthy ladies browsing the goods offered that day. Clear around the edge of the large enclosure were hundreds of posing stands about 10" tall - high enough to make the slave's genitals easy to examine; short enough to still have access to the slave's chest and study his facial features. On each stand, chained by his ankle bands, was a male slave obviously picked for his unusual handsomeness, his beautiful hair, his indisputable masculinity, his muscular, well defined physique, his flawless, usually closely shaved faces (although some had neatly trimmed short beards, usually pencil-line style), and his well-shaped sexual organs, many of which were fully erect as they were being displayed. Some retained their body hair, some were totally shaved, some had close-cropped "Marine-style" head hair; others had long, flowing locks that reached their shoulders. All were smooth shaved around their genitals, however, so nothing was hidden in that area.

As they stood in full display, the women customers fondled their bodies, hefted their genitals, squeezed their tits and balls, and, if they weren't fully erect, stroked them rather roughly until they were. Most of the women actually buying seemed to be middle aged or older, but there were plenty of younger women, even teen age girls, doing the most thorough examinations imaginable on the stock put out for sale that day. Some examinations, for example, left a slave biting his lips to keep from screaming out in agony, his chest heaving and gasping for air after being pumped to full orgasm once again, and his body soaked in sweat from the continual excitation. A few had bleeding tits from too much manipulation; a few had pricks chafed and an angry red color from being pumped one too many times; and a few were obviously pumped dry where no amount of manual manipulation would produce yet another erection, let alone an ejaculation. Many were openly sobbing, tears running down their cheeks, as they desperately tried to hide their abject humiliation and shame at the realization they were now nothing but new meat to satisfy anyone's sexual appetites that had the money to buy them. Some of the slaves, happily married and a father of children before enslavement, still couldn't imagine being marketed as a sexual toy to some jaded old woman who was so unattractive or even repulsive she couldn't possibly get a free man to fuck her under the best of circumstances, let alone have a husband desire her body. Some, early in their training, when they realized their fate, had tried to kill themselves, but the training had been so complete and thorough they now stood absolutely still with a smile on their face as a potential owner pawed and fondled every part of their body, most especially the parts they once considered private and certainly their own.

"First time here?" a deep bass voice in accented English interrupted my concentration at the lascivious scenes in front of me.

"Yes," I answered, turning to look at a handsome young man about my age, apparently a local judging from his accent, his clothing and his sun-tanned complexion. "I'm from out-of-town," I added.

"An American?"

"How did you know?"

The young man laughed. "That's easy. Your shoes give you away if nothing else. If not that, your clothing and your accent."

"Philadelphia, actually. Came down for a little shopping expedition - wanted to come here since I was old enough to read practically."

"Disappointed now that you're here?" the young man smiled.

"Hardly. It's even better than I imagined and that's saying something."

"Even those of us living here find the marketplace awesome although we can visit it every day if we want. You never get tired of the place - there's always something new, it seems. Like here, for example. I've always wanted to peek into this boutique of studs and see what was going on, but had never found the time until today. I suppose I was afraid I'd be the only male in the audience."

"So did I," I smiled warmly. "That's why I was glad to see you and a few other guys milling around."

"You can sure tell whose come off the breeding farms and those who have been here before and have been traded in on something new and different," my Brazilian companion commented.

"How?" I asked.

"Well, those from the breeding farms have been trained for this specific market for at least a year or so and know their job is to keep the ladies pleased, no matter what. They're the ones who are fairly relaxed being looked over and don't experience any shame or embarrassment at being sold as women's sex toys. For all they know, all the bucks bred back at the farm end up here and it's just what male slaves do in this world. And those that have been ladies' studs before know how to work the customers."

"Like how?" I asked, genuinely curious.

"Well, most of the women here are looking for more than just a handsome piece of meat. That's important, of course, but what's even more important is that the slave is attracted to them and can develop a romantic attachment with them. In other words, they want a stunningly handsome man who they believe will fall in love with them and be devoted to them. Romance is more important than sex to most of these women. Those studs being recycled through this market know that it's real important to get a potential buyer to believe they are turned on by her and would like nothing better than loving her - emotionally as well as sexually. Those straight from the breeding farms are taught how to give the seductive looks, the little whispers indicating attraction, and to show hard when even the ugliest old crow is handling them as if they were turned on by her and her alone. It's all part of merchandising these types of slaves and the highest prices (and the best care) goes to those who have learned how to fake romance so that even the most cynical old bat believes him."

"Jeez. You not only have to fuck them, you have to love them too!" I chuckled.

"You bet. If you don't, you'll find yourself back here for resale so fast your balls have barely had time to fill up again," my friend smirked.

What's your name, friend, if I may be so forward? I feel awkward talking this way not even knowing your name," I asked.

"Ramon. Ramon d'Salvantio. Our family owns one of the big breeding farms here - we specialize in pure blacks but are experimenting with a new line of blond-haired whites off of original Swedish stock."

"Bob Cranston here," I smiled as I shook his hand. "I own a small cell phone component assembly plant in Philadelphia and have pretty well decided to convert it to slave labor purchased here if I can find what I want. That and a couple of personal bucks for my own use," I added, letting him know right off the bat of my own sexual preferences.

"Well, Bob Cranston. We have more in common than I thought perhaps. I was sure I would be the only gay in this place selling studs to women when there are thousands of studs specifically trained for men's use just a hundred feet from here. I thought any man in here would be accompanying his wife out shopping for a dalliance when he was gone on business trips or to give him some relief when he wasn't in the mood, buying a stud for his sister or mother or niece as a thoughtful birthday gift, or..." he paused dramatically... "some one like myself just curious as to how women looked the male slaves over and what they seemed to be looking for."

"Ramon, I don't know about you, but I expected these studs to be the heaviest hung bastards I'd ever seen. After all, a stud needs to be well equipped. But some of these slaves are not much bigger than above average. Some aren't really exceptional. I expected nothing offered that was less than 10" flaccid and at least 5" around. A few are a lot bigger than that, I grant you, but look at all those that are barely 7" or 8" fully erect and probably a little less than 4" around. Aren't you surprised?"

"No," Ramon said. "You want the really big studs? Go 100 feet down to the regular sex slave market where you're hard pressed to find anything less than 11" x 5" and most are 12+ inches and so big around you can't get your hand around it. That's probably the biggest sales appeal for a sex slave to men. It seems every male buyer wants a male slave bigger than he is - psychologically it's satisfying to know you can fuck a man that's more 'man' than you are anytime you desire - it's the ultimate domination and demonstration of complete power over another human being. But women don't care as much about the stud's size. They're much more tuned in to the slave's technique, his staying power, his utterances of endearment to them when he's fucking them, him telling them how much he loves them and how much he can't live without them, and that sort of thing. His romancing and his bed talk and how pretty his face is and how much their friends envy their slave is as important in deciding to keep him as how gentle he is and being able to sustain his own orgasm until she is totally satisfied. A few inches here or there don't mean much compared to those other factors. That's one of the big differences between marketing sex slaves to women and men. My family's stud farm produces some of these guys you see up here for sale the first time and, believe you me, we've tried our best to train them around those parameters and don't pay too much attention to their prick size as long as they're at least well above average. You don't need a horse dick to make a quick selling bed buck for a woman."

"Ramon, you mentioned some of these fellows are here for resale. How are they different?" I asked.

"Look, Bob. Many of these studs are on their second or third owner. They've experienced the cycle of seeing their mistress go from wild enthusiasm and endless hours of doing everything possible to please their female owner to being abandoned as used goods and replaced with some new meat bought at this very market. Purchasers here have a way of getting bored with their new toys very quickly, no matter how much they're told they're loved and adored by a boy whose pumping his guts out trying to please them. It happens so much they expect to be traded in no matter how well they fuck - it's just a matter of time. In fact, if you go back to the holding pens, you'll hear these trade-ins bragging to each other they lasted five months or nine months with their last mistress as if the time before resale marked their worthiness in their profession."

Ramon stopped talking as we both stared at a women appearing to be in her late fifties inspecting one of the studs up for sale. First, she roughly grabbed his big balls and squeezed them until the slave bit his lip in pain and broke out in a cold sweat from the pain. Holding him tight in the grip of her left hand, she pinched his nipples until they were fully erect and continued until they were swollen and an angry red. Satisfied at his response, she left his nipples temporarily and began stroking his ample shaft, now fully erect and dripping, thrusting his hips forward as he had been taught when being handled for a mistress' convenience. She continued pistoning her tight grip on his penis until the handsome pure black bucked and gasped, whereupon she finally released his balls with her left hand and cupped her left palm in front of his throbbing penis to catch his emission as best she could. When he had completely filled her cupped hand with a load of thick, steaming cum she daintily lifted it to her mouth and drank it completely down, commenting to those around her about how thick and tangy his cum was as the slave stoically smiled straight ahead and then remembered to smile at this potential purchaser.

"That's one of ours, Bob," Ramon said. "I can tell by the brand on his right shoulder. See the Orthodox cross burnt into him - it's the mark we use to identify our farm's products. Our family is Greek Orthodox. But I remember bringing that one to market when he was 18 about seven years ago. He's been through nine or ten different owners by now, I imagine, if he's like most studs sold here. If she buys him, he's in for the ride of his life, probably. Those old ones use their studs four or five times a day. Seems like the older the old hags are, the more they want to be fucked. Someone told me it was because they need to prove to themselves they're still young and attractive. Who knows? But you see from her examination that she means business when she gets him home and in her bed."

By that time, our attention was drawn to another women looking a particularly striking young slave over. This one was with her husband apparently and they both looked the slave over thoroughly, starting with stroking his unusually large phallus to a full erection, milking him to a full discharge, massaging his balls until he moaned in despair, and then having him bend over so the husband could stick his two longest fingers all the way up the slave's well cleansed ass hole and then finger fucked him until the slave was once more fully erect.

"Oh, dear," Ramon sighed. "A double whammy!"

"What?" I asked.

"They're both going to use the stud," Ramon said. "Probably the poor slave will end up fucking the wife while he's being fucked by the husband. Sort of sandwiched in between husband and wife so to speak. It's getting to be more and more popular among the smart set here. We call studs like that 'double whammies' because two people are using their body. A 'double whammy' wears out pretty quick and is pretty well shot by 30 or so. Luckily, that boy's still nice and young - he'll last a good decade if they don't invite the neighbors in to use him too. The only problem is - studs put up for sale here usually haven't been trained for a man's use. But the stud will get used to it soon enough."

Over on the other side of the room, two teenage girls had dumped their purses on a nearby table and were carefully counting their combined money.

"Oh, Maria, we'll got just enough if some old lady doesn't try to outbid us," the youngest one said.

"Well, he's old and pretty well used," her companion added, older by about a year, but still with considerable growth ahead of her.

"Yeah, but he can still get it up and hold an erection for a long enough time. And, despite his old age," she added looking at the slave probably no more than 35, "he's still pretty good looking and has a nice big prick on him."

"Yeah, and the fact he's mixed blood probably will make him affordable. Not too many women like mixed bloods anymore, but me, I like them if they're black enough."

"Me too," the other one giggled as she reached forward and hefted the balls of the slave being discussed while her companion continued stroking the large shaft she so admired.

The slave being examined smiled stoically at the two silly girls playing with his overused organ and wondered, if they bought him, how long he could hold their interest before he was right back here being sold again, hopefully to a woman more his age. These two teenagers made him feel more a slave than he'd ever felt before, but he knew if they had the means to buy him, he could do nothing but try to please them the best he could and not be too surprised when once again he found himself in a holding cell being prepared for another auction right back here at "Mi'Lady's Stud Boutique."

"Seen enough?" Ramon asked. "I'm getting thirsty and would like to invite you to a iced coffee at my favorite bar that's right across from the main male sex slave market.

It's a great location - you can study some of the offerings chained out in front while enjoying your coffee."

"You're on," I said.   I liked the Brazilian and wouldn't mind having a local friend who knew the ropes, especially if I was going to be buying quite a few slaves here.

"Bob, you seem interested in slaves. Might you be interested in visiting my family's breeding farm when you get a chance?"

"Again, you're on, Ramon.   I've always been interested in the breeding farms, but I've never actually visited one."

"Well, high time you did, Bob," Ramon said as the two left 'Mi'Lady's Stud Boutique' and strolled across the street to the nearby bar.

"Sold!" they heard an auction master shout as the two sappy teen age girls shrieked in approval and fastened a leash to the neck collar of the 35-year-old mixed blood "old" stud as the slave studied his new owners who must have been half his age and inwardly shuttered at what lay ahead of him.

CHAPTER 7

Ramon's Background Information Really Helps

Ramon and I took an outside table close to the low platform where at least 100 male sex slaves were tightly chained in positions which showed all of their attributes off in full display. A slave waiter, a beautiful naked blond boy who looked to be about 19 or so, took our order and scurried to get our iced coffees. When he returned within the minute with our order, Ramon casually reached down, grabbed the slaveboy's balls and squeezed them tightly until the slaveboy shuddered in response. Ramon pointed to a small Orthodox Cross branded into the slave's right shoulder as the slave gasped from the ball handling.

"He's one of the first we've marketed of the new breed," Ramon said proudly. "Not fully mature yet and we probably shouldn't have marketed him this early for best return, but what do you think?"

I looked the boy/man over more thoroughly, taking in his good musculature for one so young, his fine facial features, his glowing blond hair allowed to grow shoulder length, his well shaped pecs topped by pert brown nipples, the very large balls now held tightly by Ramon, and, pushed into full prominence by Ramon's holding of his balls, his huge thick shaft, highly disproportional to the rest of his body and displayed well due to his shaved body.

"Impressive for one his age," I commented.

"Yes. We're pleased with these first ones off the line. They're so pretty they're almost feminine, yet so muscular and hung they're totally masculine. Pure Swedish stock, but highly selective, let me tell you. These first products brought a premium price when they were initially offered right across the street over there. We only had 33 of them in the first batch, but they were snapped up within a few hours. Since then, we decided to keep them off the market until they're fully mature - probably another year or so. It will cost us a little food and maintenance, but we're hoping we'll get all of that back many times over in their selling price and, of course, that extra year of training will make them even better in their master's or mistress' bed."

"Ramon, how do these bred slaves view being sold off like… well… cattle, but even more so… as whores? Any idea?" I asked. "I know free men enslaved and pressed into sex duty have to be whip trained to their new life for months and months before they accept their new destiny and even then they often deeply resent it but know there is nothing they can do about it so they eventually buckle under. But a bred slave… that's different. They never know anything else, do they?"

"No, Bob. That's why, overall, you can't beat a bred slave, especially when it comes to being a sex slave. They don't experience the humiliation, shame, and embarrassment that was taught to free men before they were enslaved and is so hard to knock out of them. A bred slave, like this boy here, has always been naked in public and always expects to be. He's always had his body handled and fondled and sees that as part of his everyday life. And, now that he's all grown up, being used sexually is no different than what he's seen every other slave he has had contact with being used. He's probably never been around anyone his age whose a slave who isn't used exactly like him. You see how I'm clutching his balls and he just stands there shuddering rather than trying to wiggle out of it. That's because he's seen that done to every other slave he knows whose worth looking at and doesn't see anything unusual in it at all - even right here in public. As far as he's concerned, that's what masters do to slaves and he's a slave, so what's the big deal? The same with fucking him. As far as he knows, all masters fuck their slaves so why should his situation be any different? It's fairly easy to train a bred slave to anything you have in mind, Bob, and you don't need much whip to back it up. The whip helps on obedience training, but you really don't need it to fight shame, humiliation, or embarrassment like you do with those enslaved later in their life."

"I know some guys that enjoy a slave's humiliation and shame when forced to do something or other. They always buy a recently enslaved boy who hasn't had much training to get the full effect - you know crying in shame, blushing bright red, and all those looks of raw hatred as they bend to the whip's demands. They claim its one of the real joys of slave ownership," I added to the discussion.

"Yes, that's why there will always be a market for the recently enslaved, especially those thrust into slavery from privileged backgrounds like you and I. Those slaves resist every step of the way into opening up their bodies for a master's pleasure and some owners enjoy the power struggle, so to speak. Of course, the slave always loses, but that's part of the enjoyment."

Ramon finally released the slaveboy's balls and he scurried, now fully erect from the handling, to another table where a new customer was being seated who, without hesitation, ran his hand around the slave's erect shaft and began playing with it until drops of pre-cum appeared and lubed the customer's hands. Only then did the customer place his order, but not before ordering the boy to turn around and bend over, spreading his cheeks so the customer could see his hole before patting him on the butt in dismissal.

Ramon and I had chuckled at the little scene. "How much do you bet that the blond is going to be ordered to the back room for a little personal inspection in the next five minutes?"

"That's a given if you mean he's going to get his butt fucked silly by that old black man," I laughed. "No bet!"

Across the street business was proceeding as usual. Numerous customers were checking out the stock items and, in the process, we could see slaves being ordered to "full display, boy, " "bend over and spread your cheeks, boy," "thrust your pelvis out more, boy," "suck my fingers, boy," "get your prick hard, boy," "milk yourself, boy, so I can see your output," and "open that mouth so I can examine your teeth with my fingers, boy."

Questions were being asked that drifted over to our table: "When were you first enslaved, boy?" "Why were you enslaved to start with?" "What breeding farm are you off of, boy?" "How many owners have you had so far?" "Men or women owners, boy?" "Are you fully trained, boy?" "Are you experienced as a bed buck, boy?" "How so?" "What did your master or mistress have you doing in bed for their pleasure?" "How old are you?" "How were you trained for your sex duties, boy?" "Any special training, boy?" "Have you always been a sex slave or have you had other duties and training, boy?" "Do you know how much your last owner paid for you, boy?" "Do you like taking a fuck or sucking better, boy?" "You ever done stud duty, boy?" "Did you stud for a mistress or master's pleasure or did you stud to produce some new slave pups, boy?" "You ever have trouble getting it up, boy?" "How many times a day can you shoot off, boy?" "How long from shooting a good load before you're ready to go again, boy?" The questions were endless and were usually paired with constant prodding and pawing of the body being questioned.

Frequently, a potential buyer signaled the market steward he wanted to "try a slave out" and the slave was promptly unchained, leashed by his collar, and the leash handle presented to the customer who quickly led the slave to the nearest available "inspection booth." Other customers, less modest and more sophisticated when it came to slave markets, simply put the hapless slave through their paces chained as they were. Consequently, a good dozen or so slaves at any given time were being fucked in place, on their knees sucking some potential new owner, or were simply being milked by a customer right in front of everyone while another dozen or so were having the same things done to them in the adjoining private booths.

"They're pretty busy today for a weekday," Ramon commented as he stared at a huge jet-black slave with a humongous erect penis being pumped to a full discharge into a four ounce paper container provided in nearby dispensers so customers could measure and taste the full load of any given slave. With a savage roar, the slave arched his back, broke into a full sweat, and began pumping volley after volley into the small paper cup until it overflowed onto the ground beneath him. The customer pumping the slave lifted the cup to his mouth and drank down a good half, smacking his lips and rolling the contents in his mouth. Seemingly satisfied, he emptied the cup in a second swallow.

"Probably buying a milk stud," Ramon commented as the black slave rapidly detumesced and his eyes began to refocus on the man drinking his 'man cream' so casually. "Some guys get almost addicted to the stuff and a good milk stud is the only answer if you can afford one. If you can find a good one, they can produce up to a full cup a day - sometimes more. A lot of protein in a stud's milk, you know." He laughed as a thought hit him. "We hear there's a new diet fad in the U.S. All the raw vegetables you want to eat and a full cup of a stud's milk every day. You loose about two pounds a day if you stick with it, we hear, and it doesn't hurt your health in any way. Have you tried it? Not that you're fat or anything, but I thought maybe that's how you keep such a good figure."

"Never heard of it myself, Ramon, but if there's a new fad diet around, you can bet my fellow Americans are hot on the trail of it. Hell, if it catches on, they're won't be enough 'milk' studs in all the slave markets of the entire world to fill the American demand," he laughed. "Maybe I better buy some before they become scarce."

"You go over to the women's market and you'll find thousands of wet nurses for sale. If that diet catches on down here in Rio, rest assured, the market across the street will make every effort to meet the demand. Every buck back in the holding pens will start training to get their production up to a full cup a day no matter what they were trained for before. Their balls won't know what happened as they start swelling being drained like that."

I thought the time had come to share my plan to buy up 70 women assembly slaves with 7 male overseer/ studs for my factory back home as well as a couple of bucks for my own pleasure. I figured Ramon could help steer me to the best bargains, be able to negotiate a 'herd' price discount, and make sure I wasn't being ripped off.

He listened to my intentions with a friend's patience. When I was completely through explaining exactly what I wanted and why, he smiled as he ordered a refill for our iced coffees. Before answering, we stared across the street once again as a magnificent Canadian slave, handsome as they come, was bent over and fucked right in front of us by a black customer from, of all places, Haiti.

"In Haiti, one percent have all the money, the others are all slaves," Ramon explained. "He could buy anything he wanted at the Haiti markets for one-third of what they cost here, but all the slaves are as black as he is. He obviously came down here to buy some white meat for his bed."

The Canadian slave was sobbing as the fucking continued, but Ramon hadn't really been distracted by the erotic scene in front of us. "I can probably get you a 20% herd discount on those women draft slaves you want, Bob, through my contacts here at the marketplace. But, for the men slaves, let's hold off until you've had a chance to visit the breeding farm. We may be able to get your seven overseers real cheap if you don't care if they're a little on the older side - handsome as you want and built for good studding, but probably well into their late thirties and early forties if what I'm thinking of is still unsold. They're some trade-ins we got recently and are really too old to bring much at market. I can probably get them for you real cheap if you don't mind some grey hair and winkles here and there. But they'd be good for what you have in mind. They've been owned all of their lives by mistresses for stud duty. They can still stud of course (and they still test out fully fertile if I remember right), but they'd make great work overseers for female draft slaves. By now, they probably would like nothing better than lording it over a women for a change, and I'm sure they'd get the last ounce of work out of those bitches if anyone would as well as keep them knocked up all the time. They'd really enjoy that, I bet!" he laughed heartily.

"That sounds great if you could arrange it, Ramon," I answered enthusiastically. "You know, you're right. Fifteen or twenty years studding to a woman's whims no matter how you feel about it and then put in full charge of some women slaves - I bet they'd get the work out of them all right!"

"As for the sex slaves you were looking for, Bob," Ramon continued. "A lot of what you see in front of you here comes from our farm, you know, but we always save some of the really exceptional back for our best customers in a private sale. They're expensive, even with the farm's discount I can pass on to you as if you were a corporate customer, but you'd have your pick of some of the best without looking all over Rio in the process. What's your preferences in that area? Black, white, tan, yellow, manly, girlish?"

"I was thinking of a black and a white, both big muscular young boys, hung well, really good looking, not too much hair on their bodies, and well trained to please a man who likes to fuck and get sucked."

Ramon broke into a huge smile and reached forward and hugged me warmly. "Bob, we're two of a kind. That's exactly what I have chained in my bedroom suite back at my city apartment. I fucked both of them right before I got dressed to come to the market this morning."

"Are your bed bucks from your breeding farm?" I asked.

"Of course, Bob. Actually, I don't own them. I've simply got them on loan. After a few months, I'll return them and pick up another two and the two I've got now will be marketed - probably right here across the street."

"Then they're not the 'exceptionals' you were talking about reserved for private sale?"

"Maybe. Maybe not. No one's classified them yet. Me. I just like the looks of them but what turns me on and what turns on some people looking for 'exceptionals' may be a little different. I like my boys to be almost brutally masculine in their looks and hung like horses. That's not everyone's cup of tea, you know."

"Jesus, Ramon. That's uncanny! That's exactly the type of slave I like. I don't know why - they look like they were made for doing the fucking - I like them because I'm fucking them."

"Exactly, Bob. Let's say it has something to do with a power trip," he chuckled.

By then an Asian slave across the street was having his tits manipulated until they were as erect as his large penis and the potential buyer, a rather puny Latino man in his fifties, was sucking away on them as he kneaded the slave's balls and shaft with both his hands. Then, much to our amazement, he knelt down baring his sagging old ass in the process. The Asian slave, well trained to pick up on customer's demands, promptly mounted the old man and began gently sliding his big prick up the withered old hole and began gently fucking him.

Ramon snickered at the sight. "As I said, Bob, you can buy a slave to do any damn thing you want these days."

CHAPTER 8

Ramon Becomes My Guide to The Marketplace

Ramon and I spent the rest of the day together where he served as a guide to all the market had to offer. By 4 PM, I was exhausted and he suggested a late lunch, very fashionable in Rio. We ate at a place outside the smells and sounds of the marketplace, which was quiet, restful, served excellent cuisine, and featured waitresses dressed in skimpy little outfits straight out of the city's famous Carnival. The waitresses were exceptionally beautiful, I thought, and commented as such to Ramon.

"Yes, I certainly agree with you there, Bob. Although they're not collared, they're slaves, of course, but carefully picked out for their natural beauty. Frankly, I think they're a lot prettier in those little costumes than if they were naked, as you'd expect for a slavegirl. I've never been interested myself, but it says here on the menu you can rent any one of them for an hour or so if you want, using the private rooms in the back of the restaurant. Most restaurants here in Rio worth anything at all offer that service, of course. They keep a cervical ring in them to prevent any unwanted pregnancies. When we're not so tired, Bob, I'll take you to a good restaurant that features all male waiters who are equally available. Those waiters are really something to look at and, like the waitresses here, usually outfitted in something that enhances their best features but," Ramon chuckled, "they're not fitted with a cervical ring. Instead they wear a packet of condoms around their neck if a woman customer wants to use them."

"I am tired, Ramon. If you don't mind, I think I'll go back to the hotel. I still think I'm suffering from jet lag and that marketplace practically did me in. I was so turned on I forgot all about how damn hot and humid the place is - sort of wears you out over time."

"And dripping until your shorts are soaked doesn't help," Ramon chortled. "I don't know about you, but my shorts are stiff with dried cum after looking at all the goodies displayed today. I think I need a good hot bath and a long night with my two boys to get things back to normal."

"Well, that too," I joined in his laughter. "I have a couple of coupons left to cash in for the hot bods available at the hotel. 'Service slaves' they call them and, from what I've seen so far, they're very appealing. Probably bought at the very market we had coffee at this morning."

"Probably," Ramon agreed. "Bob, I've got a lot to show you at the marketplace yet and, of course, I do want you to get down to the farm. How about meeting at my apartment around 10 in the morning. That way, you can enjoy both of my own boys in private while I catch breakfast. After that, we can go back for another long round at the marketplace and then eat dinner at that restaurant with the men waiters I was talking about. I'll treat for the meal if you'll treat for the waiters we choose for a little late night refreshment," he giggled.

"10AM it is, Ramon," I smiled, "but I need your address for the taxi over."

Ramon quickly handed me two cards with his Rio apartment address on one side and the family breeding farm address on the other side. He marked one card on the correct side with instructions to "just hand this to the cab driver - it's easy to find and just a short drive from your hotel. The other card you can keep if you ever want to visit the breeding farm on your own. I'll be expecting you around ten in the morning with," he added with a twinkle in his eye, "both slaves completely flushed out and lubricated for a good fucking. You'll enjoy them, I'm sure. Real beauties - one as black as midnight and the other as white as fresh ivory."

"You're quite the host," I added wryly as he insisted on paying for our dinner and we walked to the cab stand outside the restaurant. "I'm real glad we ran into each other."

"So am I," Ramon said. "I can hardly wait until I get into your pants."

"God. With all these slaves around, you're absolutely insatiable. But... I'll give your proposition serious thought," I laughed. "You present a pretty interesting package yourself, you know. The slave market doesn't have all the beauties in Rio, it seems."

CHAPTER 9

Enjoying the Service Slaves

With that, we parted. Once back at the hotel, I was so horny I was hard clear through my shower and was dripping as I picked up the phone and asked the clerk if the black chauffeur that drove the transit day before yesterday was available.

"Handy?" the clerk asked.

"Yes, that's his name," I replied.

"He's on his way, sir, and... there's a note here from the hotel manager that says his use will be free of charge... something about a complaint concerning a hotel slave. It's standard policy here. We always offer a slave's usage if there are any concerns. Enjoy Handy, sir - there's a boy that really likes to be of service in a man's bed."

Three minutes later, there was a soft knock on my suite door. When I opened it, I realized I had forgotten how really handsome and attractive the black boy was. He was fully erect just anticipating his usage and within two more minutes, I was well up his freshly cleansed ass and pumping away with abandon as the slaveboy moaned in ecstasy. When I discharged deep within him, he humbly asked if he could shoot his own load. When I said "No" he controlled his body so he didn't and inherently understood I planned to use him again forthwith. The next time I shot a load up his ass, his ass muscles were tightly gripping my shaft and rhythmically pumping me to enhance my pleasure. At that point, I gave him permission to unload which flooded the bed with pools of hot, sticky cum. As soon as he had cleaned me with his warm mouth, he quickly changed the bed with fresh linens and stood at full display as my cum dribbled down his legs, very visible on his black hide.

"Oh, all right, Handy or whatever they call you," I laughed seeing him stand there tensed up to best display his full musculature and his sexual organs, already beginning to get erect again. "You can suck me off - it will take a while - but that's it for tonight. As soon as you feel that load going down your throat and you've cleaned me off, you clean yourself inside and out in the bathroom there and then climb into the bed and I'll use you as a pillow tonight. When I wake up, I'm sure I'll want to fuck you again - at least once or twice."

"Yes, master," the slave said enthusiastically as he sunk to his knees for the ordered sucking. "Thank you, master," he added as he swallowed my organ intact and stared up into my eyes to judge my reactions to his sucking of me.

It was obvious this slave, no doubt bought at the very market I had visited today, thought servicing me to my exact demands was the most normal thing in the world. He seemed thrilled that I wasn't old and ugly and that was reward enough, no matter what I wanted done by him. The fact I had allowed him some eventual relief was a real treat for a hotel slave, apparently, and his gratitude was most evident as he gently and thoroughly sucked me clear down to the root. When I spilled another load down his throat, he promptly cleansed me off and then profusely thanked me again. Well trained he was, I thought! I wondered if all the slaves here in Rio were like this. Perhaps I should consider buying him as one of my pleasure slaves to take home. I could do a lot worse. Well, if the price was right I thought, as a freshly cleaned Handy positioned himself as my pillow and I fell into one of the best sleeps I had had in years.

The next morning I was totally refreshed and eagerly chucked down the hotel's famous "Eggs Rio Esclavo," this time sauced by an 18-year-old Ukrainian boy with long light brown hair, brilliant blue eyes, and a prick so big it really looked like it belonged on a horse, not a handsome young boy. The boy was ringed, so his genitals stood out in a most showy protrusion and his very muscular frame visibly shook in a series of tremors as he spilt an unbelievable load of very thick, tangy cum onto my poached eggs. As he smiled in success at having delivered a good load, I thought what a good milk stud he would be for those Ramon described as addicted to the stuff. I wondered if he ever thought of himself as a milk cow.

Breakfast is always the most important meal, they say, and this one had been especially good and hearty.

With a surge of energy, I got a cab and was at Ramon's apartment within minutes.

The door was opened by a splendid looking nude black boy who promptly assumed a full display position as soon as he had shut the door.

"Be right with you," Ramon called out from the adjoining bedroom as I heard some loud slurping noises and a low groan. "Just getting drained before he's all yours," Ramon laughed as I heard him zipping up his pants. Within seconds, Ramon burst into the entryway still slightly flushed and still without his shoes on. "Nothing like getting sucked dry before you hit the marketplace. Keeps you from losing your head when you see something special there. I've seen some guys all charged up when they hit the market, see all the goodies on display, and before you know it, have bought two or three slaves they needed like a hole in the head. A case of good judgment being overturned by your balls," he laughed as he slipped on some shoes. "Ah, I see you've met Rudy," he motioned to the black slave still in full display position. "He's a real hunk, isn't he, and he's marvelous to fuck, aren't you, Rudy?"

"Yes, master," the black slave answered promptly. "Anytime you want, master," he added for good measure.

"Oh, good morning, Bob," Ramon laughed. "Sergei sucks so well I forgot my manners. Tell you what, Bob. I'll grab some breakfast at the little stand by the front door of the apartment house while you sample the goodies here. Sergei, my white slave is as good a fuck as he is sucking and Rudy's good at anything you want, it seems. It'll take me a good 45 minutes to get my coffee, rolls and juice down. That should give you enough time to fuck both of these boys and do anything else you want. Just make sure you're completely drained before we hit the marketplace. If you're like me, you can't think straight with all that meat available there - better to go at this rationally with your balls completely drained to start with. Sergei and Rudy are as good as any for that - they're both products of our own breeding farm as you can see by their brands. They're going to bring top prices when we decide to sell them off."

With those instructions, he left in a whirlwind and I was left with the two gorgeous pieces of man flesh hand picked from his breeding farm. Pressed for time, I didn't dally. Rudy, the black, was ordered to all fours where I fucked him forcefully the minute I could rip my clothes off. I hadn't dog-fucked anyone in years and the experience reminded me once again how nice it was to have slaves in this world. Somehow, the position gave me a real feeling of dominance that I enjoyed so early in the morning. When I climbed off of the whimpering Rudy, I went into the bedroom where Sergei was already on his back with his legs up anticipating me. I plunged into him without fanfare for a second round and was surprised how fast I could reach orgasm again. That done, I called Rudy into the room to suck me while I played with Sergei's tits, conveniently ringed just for such use, and then, clutching Sergei's balls, milked him for another protein snack, swallowing the goods directly from its source while Rudy artfully brought me to a third orgasm for the morning and swallowed all my output down without hesitation, smacking his lips in appreciation. After Rudy cleaned my organ completely with his well trained mouth, I ordered the two to suck each other off in a 69 position since I'd only allowed Sergei to unload during his milking. Nevertheless, both slaves' needs were very evident in their quivering, dripping pricks. Smiling with delight at this unexpected treat, they quickly lunged at each other's pricks on the floor beneath me as I got all my clothes back on. Just as both slaves exploded into each other's mouths and were busily swallowing the payload, Ramon entered to witness both of the sweating bodies writhing on the floor beneath me.

"Well, I hope you didn't let them con you into giving you a little display just so they could get some relief," Ramon said threateningly at his two possessions on the floor.

"No, no, Ramon. I've fucked both of them pretty hard and the black one sucked me off after that. I just wanted a little amusement while I got dressed."

"Well, what did you think?" Ramon asked.

"I'm no connoisseur, not having a family that owns a breeding farm, but they're as good as anything I've ever fucked. Jesus, goods like this must bring a fortune on the open market."

"That's what we're hoping, Bob," Ramon laughed. "Tell me, which one did you like the best - the black or the white?" as the two slaves, exhausted, crawled to a kneeling position in front of their master with their heads bowed, cum oozing out both of their asses onto the floor beneath them.

"The black had nice warm skin that was coated with a nice, sweet smelling sheen and I liked the way he sucked me off real well - strong suctioning with a lot of tongue action. But the white boy was a lot tighter in the ass and really worked his ass muscles when I was fucking him so I wondered half way through who was fucking who. It's a draw, really. I'd pick the black if I wanted superb oral service; the white if I wanted the best fuck."

"Strange, I'm just the opposite. I like to fuck Rudy best and have Sergei wrap his lips around my shaft. Well, we'll try them both again sometime and give them another comparison."

CHAPTER 10

A Visit to the D'Salvantio Breeding Farm

"I just got a call from my uncle down on the farm," Ramon said. "He said one of our charters was down and a big shipment of slaves we planned to air freight out to a dealer in Chicago today will have to be postponed and that none of the wholesale dealers we do business with are scheduled to inspect stock today. If you want to visit the breeding farm, this would be the best day for them to accommodate us. But, if we do that, we can't take in the Marketplace today or look over any of those women draft slaves you said you could use back at your assembly plant. It's your call, Bob - I'm free either way - but I can tell you things get awful busy down on the farm sometimes and it's hard to visit properly without feeling like you're in the way."

"The farm it is, Ramon," I answered without hesitation. "I'm don't have to get back to Philadelphia for a least a week yet. How long does it take to get to your family's farm?"

"Oh, less than an hour if the traffic isn't bad. When it was first set up by my great grandfather God knows when, it was way out in the country, but now Rio has grown so much, it's practically in the city limits. But we still have all the space we need, so there's no need to move further out and it is close to the marketplace, the major highways, and the airport."

"I've had a good breakfast and I assume you had one just now. Any reason we can't head out there right now or do you need to flush these slaves out and chain them first?" I said nodding to the two kneeling slaves close by.

"I won't take a minute to chain them to their wall rings, Bob, and they can clean themselves up while we're gone. Their chains are long enough to let them reach the bathroom."

Turning to the two slaves, he ordered, "Get your asses over to the hitching ring in the bedroom and clean yourselves out good the minute we leave. You'll get fed when we get back late tonight and keep your hands off of yourself and each other. I want you both fresh and ready to serve us the minute we get back and that means, of course, I expect a hard dick and full balls on both of you. If either of you even touch each other outside of cleaning each other out, I'll put the 'Discipliner' in you and leave it for a week," he threatened. Both slaves scrambled as fast as they could to the hitching rings embedded into the wall of the bedroom close to the bathroom and waited as they were fastened by their collars to the retaining chains with lowered eyes and visibly trembling.

"Why are they shaking? Do they hate being chained up that much?" I asked, somewhat mystified since most slaves I had seen yesterday were chained routinely. Surely, they were used to it by now.

"It's my mention of the 'Discipliner,'" Ramon explained. "That's something they do hate - and probably for good reason. But it's good to keep slaves totally obedient to their masters."

"What is it, Ramon? You've got me curious now," I chortled.

"Oh, it's simple enough. Just a monster butt plug really that's covered with some interesting little nicks and picks that just torment your asshole with every move you make. A slave who has the 'Discipliner' rammed up him for a day is a slave you're not going to have trouble with ever again in most cases. It's a little treatment a slave doesn't forget and yet so easy to administer. There's one on the shelf right over there along with that assortment of whips and shackles. Take a look and you'll understand why the damn thing works so well."

I moved over to the shelf he indicated. There were a few blood stained whips of various sizes, the legendary 'cat-of-nine-tails' used for extreme correction if you didn't mind scarring the slave for life, and, easy enough to spot, the 'Discipliner'. It was a huge dildo a good 14"x6" in size, covered with tiny little plastic pins no longer than 1/16th of an inch fixed into a plastic coating textured like sandpaper. It was shaped like a typical butt plug so that, once installed, it couldn't be expelled by the recipient - a large ball shaped protrusion at the end made it hell to get pass the anal sphincter, but once in, made it impossible to expel with even the strongest ass muscles. I picked it up and found even holding it in my hands it was rough and prickly to the touch. I couldn't imagine having such a device in my anus. Even smooth, the stretching would be horrific. Rough surfaced, the pain must be … well… beyond my comprehension.

"You don't really stick this monster up a slave's ass, do you, Ramon?" I asked.

"Sure do," he answered enthusiastically, "and let me tell you, you won't have trouble with that slave again for a long, long time dependent on how long you keep it installed. The designer of this neat little device got some sort of award from the Slave Owners Society and they've sold like hotcakes. You can't own slaves and not be without one in my opinion. You'll find over at the marketplace they usually sell you one for a mere $10 with your first purchase if you don't already have one around the house. Every dealer recommends them."

As I continued to stare at the huge device, finding it hard you could stuff all of it into a slave's hole, Ramon added, "Be sure to pick one up sometime this week. They're a lot cheaper at the Marketplace than anywhere else."

"You've used it on these slaves here?" I asked almost incredulous, thinking how tight their holes felt when I had fucked them.

"Just once since I've had them, and then for just a few hours, but I've just got them on short-term loan, remember. But I'm sure they used it a lot in their training down at the farm. How about it, Sergei? How many times and how long each time?"

Sergei broke into tears and trembled all the more. "Three times, master. The first time was for an hour but the second time was all night. The third time...," he began crying uncontrollably... "the third time, master, was for all day and all night... and... master... after that, I trained real fast... and... master. I didn't need the correction after that... master."

"And you, Rudy, your experience with the best trainer in the world?"

"Just twice, master," Ruby promptly answered as he began to cry at the recollection. But the first time was four hours of hard exercise under the whip, master, so it tore my asshole all to pieces, master... It bled for two days until they could get it stopped, master. The second time they had to chain me down before they installed it, master, because I went crazy when I saw it again and tried to fight off my handlers, master. Finally, they just knocked me out and when I came to it was in me for 48 hours, master. I didn't have to move around in that I was chained down to an inspection table, master, but the stretching got so bad it ended up throbbing with each breath and hurting even more than being exercised. After that, master, I didn't need to be trained any more. I shaped up real fast after that, master, and never gave my handlers a bit of trouble after that and the trainers were real pleased with how much I had progressed. I heard them telling some new trainers how effective that special butt plug was and I sure had to agree with them."

"See, Bob, right from the horse's mouth. You'll need to get one. I'd give you that one but, as you can see, I'll probably need it sometime in the future."

Both slaves chained to the wall had a look of raw fear sweep over them at their master's last pronouncement and, unconsciously, pressed their butts forcefully against the wall as if to prevent any reintroduction of the dreaded training device.

With that, we left, hailed a cab, and 45 minutes later were at the heavy solid 20' high metal gate that served as the main entrance to the "d'Salvantio Breeding Farm" as the large bronze placard welded directly to the gate declared. The gate matched the 20' masonry walls surrounding the original 18th century farm, freshly painted with whitewash. Somehow, it looked mysterious and foreboding - perhaps because the walls and gate gave not a hint of what lay inside.

Ramon punched a 14-digit code into the gate's control as soon as the cab left us and instantly the gate opened electrically, shutting quickly behind us the minute we crossed an electric light beam which seemed to control how long it stayed open.

"This is the original farm," Ramon explained. "It's just about 400 acres, but then, of course, production was only about 10 a month or so. It now houses our accounts payable, sales and promotions, merchandising, orders, tax payments, documentation, and staff inservice training departments among others. I suppose you would call it our corporate offices, except the executives all have their offices in the new portions of the farm. Over the years we have expanded piece by piece. Now we have over 3000 acres with major sections devoted to the holding cells, training, stock maintenance and enhancement, sales, shipping, intake, and, of course, the heart of the farm, the actual breeding barns. Each section has its own design reflecting the trends at the time it was built. For example, the 50-year-old sections all feature electrified fence instead of these huge masonry walls while the latest section has no visible fences at all, but has underground cables monitoring global positioning devices implanted into all the stock nowadays. The family takes pride in keeping up with the times.

"Bob, if you don't mind, let's scurry right over to the breeding barns now. We breed four times a day normally and there's always one scheduled at 12:30 and it's 12:15 now. If we hurry, we can just make it. It's an interesting sight if you haven't seen it before."

When I nodded my assent, we quickly exited through a side door and stepped into a conveyance resembling a rickshaw with bicycle tires drawn by a hugely muscular naked white slave, now completely tanned dark brown from the unrelenting sun. His only 'clothing' was a bit fitted into his mouth and held in place by a series of leather straps around his head, his very tall slave collar which forced his head into a continual upright position, and a thick genital band fitted to thrust his very large sexual organs out in front of him in full display. A buggy whip was positioned to one side of the seat. Ramone grabbed the whip, flicked it across the slave's rump and, despite the weight of two grown men in the rickshaw, we were quickly sailing past building after building while Ramon guided the slave by tugs this way and that on the reins attached to the slave's mouth bit.

"This is one of the old studs that we've kept around," Ramon said as he flicked the whip even harder over the slave's rump. "Normally, we sell them off - usually at Mi'Lady's Boutique where there is a huge demand for old studs once we vasectomize them so they won't be knocking anyone up anymore. Mi'Lady's customers like the experience they're buying and, of course, the bodies are usually pretty spectacular, even after 10 or 15 years on the rutting benches. But we kept this one in that we needed a new pony slave here at the farm at the very time we were getting ready to sell him off so here he is. He's still good to look at, isn't he?" Ramon asked as we both looked at the magnificent body sweating and straining beneath us and took in the heavy breathing and little gasps eliminating from the slave, clearly audible back on the bench of the rickshaw.

"He certainly is, Ramon. How long did he stud?"

"Oh, about 14 years I think before his sperm count started to go down. He's been a pony slave for about 4 years now, so that would make him 37 or 38 years old now if we started him studding when he was 19 or 20. He's in good shape for an old slave like that - some of us enjoy fucking him when we're down here, but I doubt if we'll have time today. Too bad, since he's from original American stock way down the line, although he was bred here. We always keep some American breeding stock on hand in that there's a steady demand - mainly from African and American buyers. Strange, isn't it? The Africans want them because they seem to prefer to fuck well hung white stock if they can get it; the Americans like them because they look like themselves, I guess. Or at least, what they could look like if they were in top shape and had as good a gene mix as these slaves do."

"He's still good to fuck?" I responded, rather astonished.

"You bet. Keep a slave in top physical condition with good food and lots of exercise and they're as good to fuck at 40 as they are at 18. This one didn't like it much when the tables were turned and he was the one getting fucked and he sure let us know it, but the handlers fixed that fast enough. They ran him for a day under a heavy whip hitched to this rickshaw with that special butt plug, the 'Discipliner' I showed you rammed up him and after some real screaming and howling with that monster up him, he settled down. Now he can get fucked time after time and you'd never know he hates it like hell - a good training exercise can do that - teach a slave to hide any resentments he may have. After all, a slave does what he's told to do the very best he's capable of, but," he laughed, "I can see in this case there would be a little resentment. After all, he was the one doing the fucking all those years up until this new assignment. Too bad you won't have time to fuck him today. There's something special about taking an ass when you know they really hate it but they also know full well there isn't a damn thing they can do about it."

Within another minute, having woven through numerous little streets and around seemingly endless buildings and huge barn-like structures, we finally pulled up at a very modern looking facility. Ramon pulled back on the reins, drawing the slave's head back sharply as the slave gasped in pain but slowed down immediately to a full halt, gasping from his exertions.

"Well, we're here, and with a few minutes to spare," Ramon said as we left the rickshaw, the slave obviously trained to stay in place. "The rutting will get started in about five minutes if everything is running on schedule today."

"It's certainly a modern looking place for something as primordial as rutting," I laughed.

"That it is, but, for nostalgia's sake I suppose, we still use the original 18th century breeding benches with those quaint old-fashioned restraints to hold the breeding wenches in place and the antic little 'encouragement' whips they use to flick over the stud's butt once he's in action. Seems silly now with all the pre-conditioning drugs that make sure the wenches are so eager and willing, and the studs, antiseptically clean nowadays, foaming at the mouth with all that generic Viagra in them."

"I wondered if you used any pharmaceutical aids these days," I asked.

"Yes, Bob. We were one of the first breeding operations to employ them. The wenches are given low doses of fertility drugs to significantly raise the twinning rate - but not enough to yield those multiple births that led to low birth weight and poor prenatal development. They're also given a libidinal enhancement drug about four hours before breeding to make sure they're more than eager to take a stud on. Once they conceive, they're given a solid regimen of vitamins, essential minerals, and nutritional supplements to make sure they provide the best host body possible no matter what their eating habits are. We've had them try to starve themselves the first few times rather than produce a pup destined for the markets, but there's no chance of such silliness around here. After a couple of pups, they get used to the idea and we don't have much trouble with them after that. The studs are given libidinal enhancement drugs the entire time we're using them for stud - about 10 years or so before their viable sperm count starts to falter - and they also get a vitamin/mineral supplement and lots of protein that whole time. The Viagra makes sure they're always interested in their career and ready to go; the supplements make sure their semen production stays up despite the heavy demand. But that's all it takes, really."

"Ever had a stud object to baby-making for the markets?" I asked.

"Oh, every now and then - very rare, actually - but the whip takes care of that quick enough. Slaves only get philosophical on you if it doesn't hurt," he laughed. "Actually, most of them take a lot of pride in their output and keep score on how many wenches they've knocked up in their career."

We went up a flight of stairs to a luxurious air-conditioned 'observation area' that looked down over an arena of 'rutting benches' permanently in place. There were about 50 other visitors already there; mainly Japanese it seemed mixed in with a few American tourists. When we took our reserved seats up front, the place was completely full.

"We sell tickets to this through some of the travel agencies. They get snapped up real quick so we always have a full house here," Ramon explained the chatting visitors, about half men and half women, obviously excited about the scene about to unfold in front of them.

Strapped to each rutting bench below, bent far over a padded fixed bar on their stomachs to fully expose their vaginal opening with their legs wide spread, was a breeding wench, writhing and flushed in their drug-induced need.

"Same position we've used since day one," Ramon commented. "Makes it easier for the stud to get right with it; prevents the two from seeing each other's faces so they don't begin to think its anything but what it is

- two animals being bred; and the fertility rate is a little higher in this position than if they were face to face. Way back when, they designed the rutting benches like this because it made it like all other animals rutting. Since then, we realize that, unwittingly, they were also utilizing the very best psychological and physiological techniques for effective slave breeding. If you look close at the sides around their bellies, Bob, you'll see most of the wenches have quite a few stretch marks on them - a good sign in that it shows you they've had a lot of successful pregnancies long before this upcoming one. You can look at a breeding wench and see if she's any good or not at her profession by simply looking at her belly. The more stretch marks the better. A good wench can produce 25-30 pups before she wears out if she twins enough. Even if she doesn't twin much, she's usually good for 20 pups if we start her soon enough and even when she won't take anymore, she's good for another 20 years or so in the nursery raising young pups until we can put the new generation to some simple work assignments."

I quickly scanned the wenches' bellies although they were hard to see bent over the rutting benches that forced them into a totally open position for breeding. Most were covered in stretch marks and had obviously been bred numerous times before. Despite their restraints, many were trying to turn their heads around so they could catch a glimpse of what their assigned stud looked like but their efforts were in vain - their neck collars were fastened to the bench so tightly it was impossible to see anything but the wench stretched out on the bench on either side of her.

"Right on schedule, Bob. Here come the studs," Ramon said lustily, obviously already excited in anticipation of the action about to unfold in front of him.

The tourists around us broke into applause and got their cameras ready.

To my surprise, the studs weren't shackled or restrained in any way. Their resplendent bodies, covered with a sheen of sweat (obviously, only the observation area was air conditioned) were adorned only with their slave collars and the prominent d'Salvantio brand on their right butt. Each one was strikingly handsome, had a magnificent physique, and their shaved bodies revealed they were equipped as you would expect on a slave selected as a stud. They were all fully erect with their pricks glistening with lubricant. Obviously cued to do so, the studs waved at us in the observation balcony, and briefly posed for the visitor's cameras head on with legs wide apart and pelvises thrust out to fully display their genitals with a big smile on their faces, now flushed a rosy red with sexual excitement. I counted 22 of them, the same number as rutting benches; 8 full blacks, 8 whites, 2 mulattoes, 2 Asian, and 2 Arabs.

As soon as the visitors' camera flashes slowed down, the studs quickly found their assigned rutting bench, each marked with a large number. With no preliminaries, they thrust their huge organs completely into the positioned wenches who reacted with some muted screams conveying both ecstasy and agony, pumped fast and hard as the traditional 'encouragement' whip laced lightly over their buttocks administered by the rutting room's overseer (mainly to keep with the tradition, I gathered, since the whipping was so light it was almost symbolic), and within two or three minutes, each stud arched his back, thrust as deep as he could, threw his head back, and howled as he discharged deep into the wench given him. As soon as he had emptied, he waited patiently in place until the overseer squeezed his balls to make sure he had fully unloaded and slapped his rump in dismissal. With that dismissing slap, each stud pulled his huge organ out immediately (now dripping with lubricant, cunt juices, and remnants of his own cum), and, waving a quick farewell to those of us in the balcony, left with the overseer.

"The overseer is leading them to the showers where they will wash completely. Then they'll be fed and taken back to their holding cells where they'll rest up and recharge for the next stud call at around 5. They have an early morning stud call at 8 and a final one at 10 each night. We just stud them four times a day to make sure they have a full load each time, but that's their life 365 days a year. That way we get almost 1500 studdings a year out of them. The wenches will get tested 4 hours from now to see if they caught. If not, they'll be in the 5 o'clock lineup, and if they don't catch then, they'll be in the lineup again at 10. Since we make sure they're only in the lineup if they're at the peak of their fertility cycle, we only give them three chances on any given day. If they don't take then, we wait until next month's cycle before putting them to the studs again. That way, the stud's output isn't wasted. But if they don't take on the third go around, they're out of here - we throw them into the next batch headed for the marketplace. We can't afford feeding a nonproductive wench around here. That's why they reared back and bucked on the stud's pricks - they want to get fertilized if they possibly can to avoid getting sold off to a far less cushy life than just laying around here making babies."

"How many take on a single fuck," I asked, "since it's all so scientifically timed?"

"A good third, can you believe it? And another third before the allowed 8 fucks before recycling a month.

If they have to go through the second month's cycle, they earn some black marks, but by then we've generally reached a 95% catch rate. That leaves only 5% - well, it's usually the real old ones who have already produced a good 25 pups or so. They're getting worn out, but we will give them an extra month before we give up on them and assign them to the nurseries permanently?"

"And what do they do when they're in gestation?" I inquired.

"Work in the nursery taking care of the new crop of pups, work in maintenance, or do office work, dependent on their ability level. It's surprising. A woman knocked up can do most any work assigned, no matter how hard, up until about the 7th month. After that, its wise to put them into the nursery or office work just to play if safe. You don't want to lose a pup after all that investment."

"And the studs? What do they do in-between studdings?"

"Not much, actually, but we do exercise them heavily twice a day to make sure they stay in top shape. Just fucking all the time keeps their lower body in pretty good shape, but the shoulders and arms begin to sag if you don't exercise them properly. But, Bob, you know we don't have to worry about their weight at all despite the fact we feed them well. All that fucking just keeps it off of them. Just passing that on," he laughed, "since you Americans are always interested in little tips to keep the love handles off."

"And how many studs do you need to service, say, a 1000 wenches and keep all of their bellies properly swollen all the time?"

"Well, we have 5000 wenches at any given time in foal and you saw right now all the studs it takes," Ramon said.

"You're kidding, Ramon," I said. "I counted 22 rutting benches with 22 studs. Are you telling me 22 studs can keep 5000 wenches pregnant?"

"Do you math, my friend. It takes an average of 5 fuckings to get a wench knocked up, including the old worn out ones. We've got about 5000 to knock up a year. That's 25,000 breedings a year. As I said before, each stud fucks about 1500 times a year. That means we really only need about 17 studs on hand to produce 5000 new pups a year, but we always have about 5 extras around in case we run into sickness or some fertility problem with one of the studs. Besides, sometimes one of these visitors will offer us so much for a stud they've seen in action down there they'll offer us a price we can't refuse. That extra five means we can sell a few off now and then and still not have to replace them immediately. Bob, a good slave stud is a wonder to behold. Given the right circumstances, they can reproduce like crazy. And reproducing is what this place is all about. My great grandfather knew what he was doing when he built those rutting benches eons ago. But I bet he'd roll over in his grave in joy if he knew his own offspring were churning out 5000 slaves a year from those same old rutting benches. I'm surprised they haven't fallen apart by now, considering all the squirming and bucking and pounding that's taken place on that sturdy old wood."

"From 120 a year to 5000 and the quality is a lot better too, I bet," I said in admiration.

"A lot better," Ramon agreed. "The output is bigger, sturdier, more disease resistant, a hell of a lot prettier, stronger, and, anymore, most are either extremely handsome and hung like horses, or beautiful and sexy like few women you have ever seen. We can produce them in most any color you want, any hair color, any eye color. Any special features, you name it, we can produce it anymore. Selective eugenics is a wondrous thing, my friend. We've selectively bred for over 160 years now - that's eight generations of getting those genes just like we want them. I think in another generation or so, we can start thinking about a distinctive slave that we can actually market as the d'Salvantio breed: handsome beyond current standards, totally predictable as to physical and behavioral traits, and trained to lifetime guarantee standards of satisfaction. It's coming, Bob, believe me. Just two or three more generations."

"And the profits?" I couldn't help asking.

"The more slaves are being bred so successfully, the more prices come down. It's simple supply and demand despite the increased quality of the product. Nevertheless, quantity has gone up so much that even with the lower prices, you can still make a decent living. Look at this farm - 120 to 5000. Those 120 brought a king's ransom when they were sold; those 5000 are expensive but affordable so the market has opened up considerably. Despite all I've said, it's a great business to be in and one of the most promising for the future in my opinion. It won't be long until we will be able to get the price down to where practically everyone can afford a reasonable quality slave. Think what that will mean to the standard of living and all the other benefits over and beyond convenience and pleasure: no more coerced sex because you can use a slave to take care of your sexual needs, a lot less crime because with a cheap slave of your own you don't have to keep stealing to get money to buy one; a lot less mental illness and stress because slaves tend to really alleviate our stress levels for us in a variety of ways; no more power games with each other, because slaves can absorb all of those needs simply because they're there."

"Ramon," I laughed. "You're going to be a multi-millionaire if you're not already, but you don't need to make yourself out as the savior of the world too. I'll admit slave breeding is a profitable enterprise and a much needed one that significantly improves the breed through selective eugenics. And I admit a bred slave is probably a hell of a lot easier to train than turning a formerly free man into whatever you have in mind. But the world will still have plenty of problems to concern itself with; bred slaves or not. And we're still going to have free people all stressed out, date rape going on, petty crime, mental illness, and corporate power games which have turned into a sport, slaves available or not. You need to spend some time back with me in Philadelphia - you need a little reality check. You've just got too many easily compliance slaves around you all the time."

"Oh, really?" Ramon said. "Like what?"

"Well, as a start, those two boys chained to the wall in your apartment bedroom all flushed out waiting for you to fuck them upon your return; another is that pony slave standing out there in the sun waiting for our return trip and, if we have time, a good fucking from the two or us. Shall I continue?"

"You're complaining?" Ramon laughed. "You Americans are crazy."

"Notcomplaining-enjoying," I laughed even harder. "It's just I wished I lived here instead of Philadelphia where we don't have breeding farms supplying the local markets with all these reasonably priced, fully compliant goodies. Maybe I've missed my calling. Instead of jacking out cell phone parts to make a modest living, I should be cranking out slaves by the thousands and making some real money. Ramon, you've opened my eyes to the real reality in today's world."

"Maybe you'll get your wish - at least part of it," Ramon said mysteriously with a strange look on his face. But then, the jocular look returned and he said, "Now I understand you. For a while there, I thought you had wandered off into lulu land. Now you mentioned that American buck standing outside sweating in the sun. Still interested, Bob?"

"You bet, Ramon. That was one good looking hunk of meat and," I paused dramatically, "I don't think I've ever had a 38-year-old piece of ass, especially of American stock."

"Well, high time you did, Bob," Ramon chuckled as led me out of the observation room and back to the waiting rickshaw. The noisy tourists we slithered through were still excitedly sharing their digital images of the event with each other.

CHAPTER 11

The Studs' Holding Cells and
Touring the Rest of the Farm

Out of the air conditioning, the heat was unbearable as the Brazilian afternoon got into full steam. The patient pony slave was waiting in place in the boiling sun, sweat pouring off his body.

"You want to drive, Bob?" Ramon asked, tossing me the reins and the light whip. "Don't worry - I'll tell you where to go and the pony here knows most of the destinations anyway."

I took the reins and pulled them back sharply. The slave's head jerked back and I heard a muffled scream despite his mouth bit.

Ramon laughed. "Just takes a light touch. The reins are mainly to indicate to him which direction to turn. The whip's a lot better to start him out and to speed him up."

With that, I loosened the reins until they were slack and aimed the whip at the slave's butt with a light snap of my wrist.

"Ahhhhh…" a retching scream emanated from the gagged slave as we lurched forward throwing both Ramon and I back against the seat.

Unconsciously I again pulled abruptly back on the reins in an attempt to stop. The slave's head snapped back as far as his tall neck collar would allow and the bit cut cruelly into the corners of his mouth as we stopped as suddenly as we had started. I looked down and the slave was choking and screaming simultaneously behind his bit/gag while his butt was bleeding where the whip had torn open his skin.

Ramon was doubled up in laughter. "You're like a 16-year-old just learning to drive a shift car who can't master the clutch," he sputtered out between peels of laughter. Here, let me drive while you study the technique and then, I promise, I'll give you the reins again. At this rate," he laughed even harder, "we'll never get there before the slave's torn to bits."

Ramon took over, not paying the slightest attention to the slave's predicament, and whisked the whip lightly once more over the slave's butt while he held the reins loose. We moved ahead smoothly and accelerated rapidly.

"See, easy does it," he chided. "A light touch is all that's needed with a trained pony. The whip is really only to give signals with, unless you really want to speed or you're going up a steep hill or pulling an extra heavy load. Then, of course, a steady whip and even a pretty heavy one, is necessary, to get everything out of the slave he's capable of."

"If you're not worn out yet, I thought while we were here I'd show you the stud's holding stalls so you could examine them up close after they've cleaned up. We'll skip the delivery room - we almost always have at least one of the wenches birthing at any given time but its messy and pretty bloody and a woman's not looking her best when she's birthing a new pup. Instead, we'll take a peek at the nursery of new pups. After that, we can swing by the shipping department so you can see how we send the wholesale shipments out by airfreight. To see everything would take a week or so, but we can do what I mentioned if you're willing to stay until 8 or so today. We can take late lunch right here in the executive suite as sort of a break in all this."

"Sounds good," I said, studying the muscled butt of the slave in full action as he swiftly pulled us at an astonishingly brisk trot.

Ramon saw me studying the slave's ass. "I know I promised you some of that ass, Bob, but right now isn't the best time unless you like your slaves all hot and stinky. He can clean up while we're having lunch and we can fuck him for dessert," he chuckled. "Although," he paused, "my guess is that some of the waiters may turn you at lot more than this old stud."

The slave being discussed blushed beyond that caused by his exertions so it was obvious he was listening to our conversation despite his increasing difficulty taking in enough air to offset the demands being placed upon his body. He was well beyond heavy panting now and was into gasping and his body was literally dripping showerlets of sweat. But the blush of humiliation at being offered so casually to this newly arrived foreigner was still evident. He had no time to reflect on this before he felt the reins forcing his head painfully back as a signal to stop. They were at the place he had called home for 14 years - the stud's holding stalls - and the two young masters left him deserted once again, wheezing and gasping trying to fill his lungs back up.

Ramon led the way into the well lighted interior where there were 22 identical stalls, fresh straw on the floor and open on the side facing the center aisle. Inside, chained only by their ankle band to a ring in the wall of the stall, were the same 22 that had seen in action just a few minutes before, still dripping wet from their recent shower and now quietly munching a fresh ration of slave chow dispensed in a bowl hung chest high from the stall's walls along with a water bowl similarly attached. The slaves glanced at us briefly as we entered and, leaving their food temporarily, positioned themselves at the front of their stalls, hands clasped to the back of their slave collars and feet spread wide apart with their pelvises thrust out. It was obvious they were well acquainted with visitors in their quarters and were used to being inspected.

"Look them over, Bob," Ramon invited as he went to the first stall and hefted the huge penis of an Arab stud up in the palm of his hand. The Arab was, by anyone's standards, one of the best examples of masculine beauty available. Tall, muscular, galvanizingly handsome with long black eyelashes and a beautiful creamy tan complexion with deep black eyes, he was built so that every muscle was well defined. His sexual equipment was huge but well shaped and seemed to invite handling.

"Most of these boys were bred right here at the farm and, when we saw how well they were developing, held back for stud as the very best of the crop. That way each generation of studs just keeps getting better and better in what we're looking for in genetic traits. These are the best of the best so to speak so its fun to look them over - kind of a quick view of what breeding is all about. But a few, like this Arab boy here, we've bought to get something we didn't have around or because they seemed to be even better than our own stock in one aspect or another." He began to stroke the Arab boy until the stud's giant penis rose to a full erection despite its recent workout. "Most of them are bred slaves themselves whether we raised them or we bought them from a dealer somewhere, but five of them in this crop are 'first generation' slaves - that is, they were enslaved long after they were born. This Arab boy here is one of those," Ramon continued as he accelerated the stroking until the young man was dripping. "After this boy's family was wiped out in the war in Afghanistan, he was quickly captured by some slave traders in the region of his mountain home when he was 18, but fully mature. Afghanistan has always practiced slavery, of course, and the recent wars have only added to the available supply through prisoners of war, war orphans, the refugee homeless, and the desperate. Ironically, he was sold to an old Kurdish man - the Kurds were his tribes' most hated enemies - who used him for his heavy work and as a fuck boy until he was sold again to a traveling slave dealer when he was 19 where he ended up on the auction block at the country's largest slave market located discretely right outside Kabul.

That's where one of our agents spotted him who thought he could be trained as a stud here. The agent was right. This boy took to studding like a real natural and actually was grateful to be here. He hated that old Kurd master who fucked him every night and it was mutual - that's why the Kurd sold him to the dealer so quickly. He fought the old man every time he was bedded despite being whipped for his insolence and, in the moment that decided he was to be sold, actually spit in his master's face when he was being taken for the third time that night. The story goes he didn't mind sucking the old man off much, but he hated being fucked, claiming it made him less than a man. The old man whipped him raw, even threatened to castrate him, but he still wasn't very cooperative. When he spat at the old man, that broke the camel's back and he was sold off to the next itinerant dealer that came by.

Here he claims we don't ask him to do anything a real man doesn't do anyway and we've never had a bit of trouble with him. He's always ready to do his duty and doesn't seem to care who or what he's put to. He must be smart too - he's picked up a good working knowledge of both Portuguese and English just from listening to the handlers. He can understand every word I've said," Ramon said as he moved his hand down and began churning the slave's balls, still soft and spongy from their recent draining, as he addressed him directly.

"You like it here, boy?" Ramon asked the Arab slave.

"Yes, master. This good home for slave. Your slave like making babies for you, master," the slave answered sincerely.

"Well, keep making those babies and we won't have to sell you off to some old man who will want you for his bed. A pretty body like yours shouldn't be wasted, slave boy," Ramon responded as he tweaked the slave's tits with his other hand after running his hand completely over the slave's upper body. "Remember, Allah gave you this magnificent body so you could share it with others."

"Yes, master," the Arab slave responded with lowered eyes humbly. "Like you say, master, it was God's will I was made a slave, master."

"Undoubtedly, slave. Inshallah! Otherwise, your good fortune wouldn't have placed you here in my possession."

"Praise be to Allah!" the slave responded enthusiastically as he thrust his huge ballsac further into his master's hands as a sign of his complete submission to Allah's will.

Bob stared at the Arab slave's total acceptance of what had happened to him. He couldn't believe that a boy once free could so easily have adjusted to becoming the possession of whoever had enough money to buy him, even gleefully taking on the role of making new slaves four times a day 365 days a year and standing there submissively while a 'master' as young as himself played with his sexual organs right in front of everyone without a glimmer of resentment or shame.

"Bob, here's the stud I really wanted you to see as he strode down to the 8th stall and roughly grabbed the prick of the young man standing in full display there. "This one too has only been a slave for two years altogether now. Before that, he was a auto mechanic in a small town in southern Alabama."

I stared at a rugged looking mountain of muscle with a creamy white complexion, blondish hair and deep blue eyes. He was handsome beyond description, built like a bull, and hung like a horse. His body was totally shaved below his eyelashes and he was distinguished by a thick copper nose ring fitted into the septum separating his two nostrils matched by copper rings fitted to each of his large tits, giving him a somewhat animalistic look. He looked to be in his early twenties.

"The Americans we've put to stud here have worked out well," Ramon explained as he pulled the slave out of his stall by his prick as far as his retaining chain would allow. "And we're counting on that holding true in the future as well," he added, again with that strange mysterious look he got.

"You say he was enslaved only two years ago?" I asked, wondering how a small town white boy from the South ended up a slave in a Rio stud barn.

"Yes, Bob. His hobby used to be weight-lifting and he had entered himself in a regional bodybuilding contest in Macon that one of our 'spotters' attends occasionally looking for new stock. This boy caught his attention so he visited him back in the 'prep rooms' claiming to be an agent for a modeling agency. There he was able to see all of the boy in the showers and, liking what he saw, interviewed the boy extensively. Turns out the boy had no wife or family (his parents had died a few years earlier), only a part-time job where he wouldn't be missed if he didn't show up, was completely directionless in his life, and essentially broke. In other words, perfect for a slave hunter. The spotter then found out the boy spent most of his time "chasing pussy" as he put it, had fathered several children illegitimately already even though he was only 17 then, and claimed almost all women and a lot of men were always after his "great body and big dick."

"Within an hour, that boy had drunk a beer full of knock out drops and woke up stark naked a day or so later in a holding cell here at our training barn. It took some chronic hunger, a lot of the whip on that pretty back and rump, and the 'discipliner' up his hole repeatedly before he realized his life as he knew it back in Alabama was now over and, from now on, he was a piece of property owned by a breeding farm in Brazil. He held out a little while until it was clear to him that no one was going to be looking for him - in fact, no one gave a damn that he was gone, even if they had noticed his absence. When he realized we were going to take care of him if he shaped up to our demands, and if he didn't he was going to spend the rest of his life with that special dildo up his ass, he began to come around amazingly fast. Fitting him with the nose ring and having the trainers fuck him a few times also helped drive home his new reality. After he was fully trained in just three or four months, we brought him over here where he was delighted when he found out his new assignment was, as he so delicately put it, 'fucking pussy all day'" He's been here ever since just pumping out new pups four times a day." By this time, the American's prick had grown to full length in Ramon's hand and was beginning to jerk around a bit in its excitement.

"Easy, boy," Ramon laughed as he looked at the pulsating prick in his hand. "There'll be more pussy for you to fuck in just four more hours."

"Yes, master," the gorgeous blonde said gratefully in a thick southern accent, his nose ring bobbing from the movement of his upper lip as he spoke.

"Why are we giving you the privilege of fucking all these beauties?" Ramon asked the American slave, obviously for my benefit.

"To make babies for you, master," the slave answered brightly. "Look at the chalkboard, master, over there on the wall. I've scored 842 times now, master."

"That's good, boy, considering the time you've been here. But remember, slave, that's the only reason you're here. If you stop scoring, you're up on the auction block, boy, just like any of the other studs."

"Yes, master," the American slave said humbly, seemingly unworried that he would ever run out of fertile juice or ever find himself unable to get it up and perform appropriately anymore.

"You like it here, boy?" Ramon asked as he let loose of the rampant prick and grabbed the slave's nose ring to look him directly in the eye.

"Yes, master. I like to fuck. Just born to fuck pussy, I think, master."

"Anything you don't like, slave?"

"Not really, master, once those trainers stopped fucking me. Only thing, master, is I get lonely sometimes. Most of the other studs don't speak in English much and I wish there was someone for me to talk to sometimes, master. I don't know if those women we fuck speak English or not, master. We don't get much chance to talk to them," he smirked, "if you know what I mean. Be nice to have a nice Alabama boy down here with me, master," he suggested.

"Well, I don't know about an Alabama boy, slave - we probably couldn't stand to hear two or you talking in that 'good ol' boy' Southern drawl, but we might be able to arrange another American stud one of these days."

The young blonde brightened up with enthusiasm. "Really, master? That would be wonderful, master. Give me someone to talk to when we're sitting around or exercising recharging our balls getting ready to fuck again, master."

"You planning to buy an American slave to stud, Ramon?" I asked.

"We've got one in mine, Bob," Ramon replied lightly. "Now, unless you wanted to finger some of these other studs, we should skedaddle over to the nursery."

CHAPTER 12

A Training Battalion Passes

Just outside the stud's holding cells, the pony slave awaited us dripping in sweat from the blinding heat of the sun. As we climbed aboard, a large cadre of male slaves looking to be about 19 or 20 went trotting by, linked by chains to their neck collars with a couple of trainers on each side with long whips riding alongside them in slave-drawn rickshaws similar to our own. The clinking of their chains and the cracks of the trainer's whips echoed off the buildings on either side as the slave's panting and gasps formed an interesting background noise. The young slaves all stole a glance at us as they quickly passed, seemingly always eager to see anything new in their rigidly scheduled lives.

"They're nearing the end of their training," Ramon said, "before being marketed. By now, most of them are eager to be sold - it will be a whole new life for them."

I looked at the naked slaves as they passed row after row after row. Judging from their physiques and sexual organs, most of them were well into manhood or nearing completion. Already they were completely body shaved, but the stubble on some showed they would have hairy bodies if left untended. Despite the fast trot, they were forced to maintain by the cracking whips over their backs and rumps, a good many were still at least semi-erect indicating they probably weren't allowed to masturbate or otherwise relieve themselves in readying themselves for the marketplace. I could imagine them at rest - it looked like the majority would be showing hard at this level of need.

"How many are in this bunch?" I asked incredulously. "It looks like there must be thousands."

"A thousand in a batch. We've found that's the best number for economy in training. Any more and a few learn the trainers can't keep track of them all in disciplining them. Any less and the trainers get too zealous and some of our property gets damaged with excessive use of their whips and other training devices - especially use of those 'discipliners.' We used to run them in battalions of 500, but too many asses got torn up in training them - turned out the trainers had too much time on their hand and were inserting them up the boys' asses just for something to do, I think. With 1000 in a training corps, they don't have time for that except for the cases where use of the 'discipliner' probably is called for. Bob, our trainers have to have an eye on them too or our property gets damaged. Sometimes, their enthusiasm to turn out a perfect product just gets over the top. But we've pretty well stopped the worst of it now. They get docked the full cost of a slave every time anyone in their charge dies or is damaged to where we can't sell him to anyone but the drug companies as a test subject and you know they don't last long there."

Well, I didn't know. I didn't even know that's how the drug companies tested their drugs but let the matter drop for now. "Ever bred a slave who can't be trained?" I asked.

Ramon stared at me as if I had lost my mind. "I could see a question like that if we were talking about a boy newly enslaved, but bred slaves? I think we've had a few newly enslaved beat to death by the trainers because they were a little slow learning things, but very few actually. And we've had one or two newly enslaved over the years go crazy on us - we call them rogue slaves down here - but there's still a market for them. Slave trainers buy them as a challenge and utilize them as a recreational hobby - it's called 'slave breaking.' They have contests, prizes, and everything. But bred slaves? I can't think of a one. Remember, anyone less than perfect in body is usually aborted long before they're even born so there aren't any defects that way. And bred slaves never know anything else but absolutely obedience to a master - it's all they ever witness in their lives. Even the slightest disobedience always leads to punishment and pain - it's all they know from the day they're born, so by the time they're like these boys in forced exercise marching by here, the thought of being anything but a piece of property being prepared for the auction block is incomprehensible to them. You'd be hard put to convince them otherwise at this point. Train a child right and he's trained for life is an old saying that's absolutely correct and these slaves here prove it each and every day of their lives. Even when they're 60 years old, if a slave is lucky enough to last that long, these boys will be totally obedient to any demand of whoever owns them then and doing their damnest to please their owner, no matter what he or she wants them to do. 'Go fuck a pig, jump off a cliff, get down on the floor so I can walk on you, bend over so I can stick this 'discipliner' up your ass, rake leaves until you drop from exhaustion, eat this garbage, suck this pussy, eat this dick,' doesn't matter, they will do it with a 'thank you, master,' as the automatic response. That what a d'Salvantio product is all about, Bob."

As soon as they passed, the smell of their sweat filled the air as the sounds of the whips got dimmer. I noticed our pony slave now had a huge hard on. Pointing to the slave's condition, I asked Ramon: "Nostalgia for when he was that age here, or do you keep him so hard up even some sweaty chained-up boys in training turns him on?"

"More of the latter, I imagine, Bob," Ramon chuckled. "He probably hasn't been allowed to unload in over a month and, considering when he was a stud he unloaded four times a day whether he wanted to or not, you could see where he gets to the point where if a turtle walked across the road, he would get a hard on - and it wouldn't even have to be a female turtle anymore."

The slave being discussed blushed deeply, but the strained look on his face as much as admitted as what his master was saying was true.

"Wait till we fuck him, Bob. You won't get half way in him before he'll start shooting all over the place no matter how much we tell him not to. Just the slightest stimulation and he starts spouting all over the place," Ramon said. "Just a damn animal."

The pony slave blushed even deeper, but again a renewed quiver of his erect prick and the appearance of a drop of pre-cum on its tip gave away the truth of his master's words. If 14 years serving stud in public four times a day on command didn't prove he was an animal, certainly being hitched up as a naked pony to a rickshaw with a bit in his mouth like a donkey proved the point. Showing hard right in public when a group of young slave boys parade by was exactly what a stud horse who hadn't had a mare in months would do. Yes, he was an animal as his master claimed.

CHAPTER 13

The Initial Training Facilities

A short journey in the rickshaw took us to a whole new section of the farm comprising 24 separate buildings identified only by numbers 1 through 18, each followed by an M or an F. As we went to the entry to the first building, Ramon explained.

"We have a nursery for each year the puppies are old and we keep the two genders separated from birth on so they don't get used to each other. Since we're in such a rush, I thought we'd limit our visit today to some 18-year-old male pups in that they're already put to work. We won't have time to look at them all. Remember, we're producing 5000 a year for the market now."

"What about the female slaves?" I asked.

"We keep a few - the very best - for breeding stock so they don't go anywhere. But most of them are sent to the training barns around 18 or so and then shipped to market as soon as they're physically fully mature around 20 or 21. We could sell them off when we can legally prove they are 18 - but we get the best return on our money if we keep them until they are in the full bloom of maturity and fully trained for complete sexual satisfaction as well as any one of a hundred other duties female slaves are in hot demand for: waitresses, secretaries, nursing, nannies, housekeepers, assembly line work, farm helpers. But whatever, if they're decent looking, they're being bought to fuck as well as work and so they're fully trained to satisfy anyone in that area: both men and women."

"Women buying female slaves for sex?" I asked, almost indignant.

"Bob, you are naive. You'd be surprised at the market there. What did you think, only gay men satisfied their needs with slaves? You said you were in the market for a couple of bucks to fuck? What made you think women with a bend would be any different? Or, just like men purchasers, women who were just looking for a little variety in their sex lives?"

"I just hadn't thought about it," I said sheepishly. "I suppose if I can buy up a boy or two to play around with, a women can do the same with a girl."

"Of course," Ramon said. "It's who profits from it that counts. That's why our training is so complete."

By the time our conversation was over, Ramon and I were entering one of many huge buildings, this one prominently marked '18M.'

Here, it was almost eerily quiet considering the huge number of slave boys inside. All that could be heard was the whir of some huge fans near the roof, the occasional crack of a whip followed by the high-pitched scream of some unlucky recipient, and the slight shuffling of bare feet and asses as the slave boys worked feverishly away assembling flat-screen TV sets. Each boy stood in back of the assembly bench so he could work freely, although he was shackled to the bench by a short chain attached to his ankle band. But what was unique was a short flexible wire sticking out of each boy's ass. Save for their tight slave collars, each boy was naked.

"What's the wire thing sticking out of their ass?" was my first question of Ramon.

"Our latest invention, Bob," Ramon answered enthusiastically. "It's a metal butt plug that's a wireless shocker. If the boy slacks off or lets his attention wander from what he's doing - you know how 18-year- olds are - the overseer behind that console over there just hits that slave's button and a good sized shock goes right up that slave's ass. From their reaction, it must really be something because they act like they're being fried in the process, but it only lasts a few seconds so it doesn't really hurt anything. But it sure keeps their minds on what they're doing and has upped production a good 40% since we jammed the little devices up them on their work shift. Better yet, if the inspector finds a defect in their assembly work, they get a 30-second shock session after the error has been pointed out to the slave boy so he knows what he did wrong. You should see them taking a shock that long, Bob. They pull back as far as they can to get away from the shock to the point where the ankle band actually tears into their flesh a little but the little show is instructive for the other boys, of course. A slaveboy getting the 30-second shock never makes that mistake again, they say, so quality has shot up as well. It's a wonderful invention - the chief overseer over there behind the console is the one who thought it up and worked out the design details. Before, he had to whip hell out of the boys to keep them at it properly. Now he can just sit there and save his strength. End result: more TVs made with better quality; overseers not all worn out whipping slaves all day; and bodies not all marked up from disciplining which lowered their market value."

"How can they piss like that, shackled to the bench?" I asked.

"Well, in place, Bob. We hose the place down at the end of every shift anyway so it doesn't matter too much. We've always had that feature here, long before the wireless butt plug. It saves wasting production time on toilet breaks. Few slave occupations allow time off for pissing anymore. We also water them in place with no trouble - a close-to-worthless over-the-hill slave in his 60s or 70s can do that easy enough and these boys can shit before and after their work shift on their own time."

"Do they eat in place too?

"Don't need to. They only work an 11 hour shift - that's the way slave work schedules are set for slaves this young. They eat a good breakfast before being shackled and eat again after their work shift is over. That's enough for slaves this old. They can eat all they want each time, and you wouldn't believe how much slave chow they stuff down each time since they burn up a lot of calories in their work shift - all they do in their off-time is eat, shit, and do forced exercise for a hour before showers and bed to make sure their bodies are kept in top shape."

"You're working these boys on their feet at top effort for 77 hours a week?" I asked.

"Yes, I know it's a light work schedule for slaves well into their manhood, but Bob, you have to realize we're simply working them to prepare them for market. The TV manufacturer we've contracted with wants them working 13 hours a day like most slaves in this age range, but we won't allow it. It cuts out the feeding, exercise and sleeping times so they don't develop as fast for market. After all, we're producing top quality slaves here for the marketplace, not to just build TV sets. But most TVs sold in the States these days are made by slaves working up to 15 or 16 hours a day under a heavy whip. Those slaves are just bought to make TV sets their whole lives, so no one gives a damn about their market value. Its obvious when you look at them when they're up in their late twenties - all stooped over, the musculature of their lower bodies almost spiderly from lack of exercise and generally worn-out looking due to lack of proper sleep and nutrition. Besides that, by that time their bodies are just a mass of scars and weals from the overseer's whips. They don't have the advantage of the wireless butt plugs," Ramon declared pridefully. "We've kept that little secret to ourselves."

"I can see where the d'Salvantio operations are way ahead of the competition," I replied, indicating I was getting tired and it was time to move on.

"Ready for the final training barns?" Ramon asked, getting my hint that I was satiated with the farm's initial training operations.

"Yes, although it's obvious a significant amount of training takes place right here if this building is any example."

"Exactly," Ramon said, pleased at my response. "That's why we wait until the slaves are fully mature before we put them into final slave training which prepares them for the demands of the marketplace. It only takes 4 to 6 months on the average."

"What's left to teach them?" I asked.

"Oh, slave manners like the proper verbal and behavioral responses to a new master, getting used to being examined by strange people, little tricks to up their value in the auction bidding like posturing, smiling, showing hard, and things like that, but most of all, Bob, learning how to provide all the sexual services demanded of slaves today. We train them in all sexual acts that will be demanded of both women and men buyers. After all, we have no idea of who will be buying them - an old man just wanting to be sucked off; a young buck who's going to be fucking them five or six times a day; a middle-aged dowager looking for a stud to show off to her friends and to fuck her silly every night; a young divorcee wanting to whip a man to vent her frustrations; an executive looking for a slave to fuck him. Who knows who will buy him or for what purpose? We prepare a D'Salvantio slave for any eventuality and to handle it with class."

With that injunction, we headed back to the sweating pony harnessed to the rickshaw and soon were zooming to the training barns, located some distance away.

CHAPTER 14

The Final Training Barns

Basic training only takes around three or four months for a slave bred here because of all they've learned in the nurseries while they were growing up, but the newly enslaved that we've obtained take around six months usually," Ramon explained as we entered the vast building. "We can't begin to visit all of the training stations here but we can visit one or two of most interest to you. Remember, a good part of the training for the slaves bred here has to do with market preparation and getting them acclimated to their upcoming sexual duties once they're sold. For the newly enslaved, it takes about two months to break them to their slavery before we can enter them in the usual training programs preparing them for market."

"All of it seems interesting, Ramon, but I've always been most interested in how you teach those newly enslaved to take to being fucked regularly as well as sucking off their new masters willingly. It seems once they're doing that, it's proof they've accepted their slavery pretty well. The other part that intrigues me is breaking in your bred slave stock to being fucked regularly without putting up much of a fuss about it. Hell, most of them at the hotel even thank you for fucking them."

"Bob, you're right in identifying two separate processes for getting to the same result - a willing piece of flesh to satisfy a master's dick. Let's visit the training station where the newly enslaved are being introduced into their sexual duties. After that, we can drop over to the station where those bred right here are being initiated," Ramon suggested.

We walked some distance to the station that specialized in the newly enslaved young male stock. I was astonished when we entered. Chained tightly belly down over waist-high saw horses were about a dozen well muscled slaves with every hair on their bodies shaved off. Their backs and butts were striped with angry whip welts, just short of lacerating the slave's hide. Their legs were chained wide apart so their hole was easily available. The stench was overpowering - vomit and piss lay below each slave as he had reacted to the intense pain he was enduring, but his shit was held in place by a huge dildo inserted well up into his anal chute Their screams of agony were muted by the penis gag forced well down their throat held in place by straps reaching around their head - they were thin enough to allow breathing and vomiting, thick enough to stretch the throat and mute the shrieks of pain. Recent d'Salvantino Farm ownership brands were still red and weeping on each slave's right butt while a shiny new collar was locked tightly around their necks. Currently trainers behind each slave were plunging the dildos forcefully in and out of the slave's hole with one hand while snapping a short silk-corded whip which strung terribly but didn't break the skin over their shoulders and ribs. The slaves were, in essence, being raped by a dildo - a rape that never seemed to end judging from the sweat on the trainer's faces and the hoarse groans coming from the slaves that had probably once been screams of terror but were now too exhausted to scream properly. Most had trickles of blood seeping out of their holes with each plunge of the dildo into them.

"We just do this two hours a day to start with," Ramon explained, "until their ass toughens up. At first, they're so sore they can't walk, but after a month or so, they're stretched enough so they can take even the largest dildo without screaming - it's the whip they're feeling then despite the fact a slave's body eventually builds up some tolerance to the pain of the whip. The rest of the time we exercise them, keep them on short-ration so they're chronically hungry, give them a chance to see those already through training taking a good fuck and sucking the trainers off without any protest, and informing them they can cut their time with the dildos and get more slave chow if they volunteer to suck off the trainers.

The rest of the time we teach them basic slave manners, proper forms of address, letting them get use to being naked all of the time, and letting them know their life is permanently changed and there's no going back ever to being free. Within a month of this, they've pretty well accepted their slavery; within two months most of them realize they don't own their own bodies anymore; and shortly after that, they accept being used in about any fashion you can think of. At that point, there's no need to shackle them anymore or use the whips and dildos. They respond to their trainers' commands and just bend over and spread their ass checks when they're told to take a fuck and get down on their knees and open their mouths and swallow when they're told to suck a trainer off. By three months, most of them are eager to get fucked or swallow down a big one - they know that's the only way they are going to be fed properly and to avoid the whip on their back. The final step is getting them to thank you for fucking them of having them suck you off. When they do that without prompting, you know they're trained properly. If any of this doesn't happen exactly on schedule or before, we simply use the 'discipliner.' Once or twice with that thing up your ass and a slave completes his training real fast."

"Ramon, it's sort of smelly in here," I commented, holding my nose while studying the look of absolute despair and desperation on the tear-stained faces of the tightly constricted slaves being trained.

"Bob, you'd be stinking too if you had been free up until last week," Ramon laughed, "and only thought all these things happened to someone else. But I see your point; we'll now go to the station where the bred slaves take all of this in stride."

Ramon was right. The bred slaves straight from the nurseries were on their hands and knees without a shackle in sight, their backs free of any recent whip marks or burns from an electric prod, calmly accepting some pretty big dildos being gently eased into their well lubricated holes. The only sound were some low moans as they wiggled their asses around to better accommodate the trainer's efforts, aided in part by the trainer's other hand slowly stroking their pricks to effect a full erection while the other hand was steadily pushing the dildo up their hole until it was massaging the slave's prostate and the slave responded by shooting a huge load all over the floor beneath them. The minute they ejaculated, they were congratulated on their accomplishment, reminded to thank the trainer for 'fucking' them, and the dildo was removed until another time when the slave had had time to recharge.

"Simple Pavlovian conditioning," Ramon explained. "They associate sexual pleasure with getting fucked. Once they get the connection, they never forget it. You can see where a well-trained slave actively seeks out getting fucked - you probably witnessed that over at the hotel."

"Sure did," I replied. "And I can now understand why they thank you for fucking them. It's clever training, I admit. But what about being so eager to suck a master off?"

"That's not hard, Bob. First, we lace their slave chow with some fresh cum so they get used to the taste and associate it with being fed and taken care of. Then we cut their rations so they're really hungry all the time to the point where they just get desperate for anything to eat. At that stage, we give them a small container of fresh cum we've drawn out of some trained slaves and tell them it's the best, most satisfying snack in the world. We point out it's called "man milk" by connoisseurs around the world who are after the very best supplement for building up your body and satisfying hunger. After that, we let them know the only way they're going to get anything to eat is to suck some fresh cum out of their master, if he so honors them and allows them the privilege. It's not long until they're on their knees begging their masters for some 'man milk' and after that, it's all a matter of teaching them a master's preferences in yielding his 'man milk' - technique, in other words. The glory of this system is you have no problem with them swallowing the cum - after all, swallowing it is what they want."

"Ingenious," I retorted. "That explains why your boys at the apartment this morning as well as the whores at the hotel all seemed so damn eager to wrap their lips around my prick and stay there until I had delivered a full load down their throats. And," I laughed, "each and every one of them did thank me for the privilege. I didn't realize I was literally feeding them."

"Speaking of which, it's time for lunch over in the executive suites. I imagine you're about famished by now."

"Well, it is 4 o'clock, Ramon."

Again, we jumped back in the rickshaw and were speedily taken to the most luxurious building on the grounds. As I studied the pony slave panting away in front of us, his buttocks undulating with each step, I reflected on all the training he had gone through over his many years. Now with some grey hair beginning to show around his temples, I could well imagine him sitting before a trainer when he was 19 or so learning how he too could get some 'man milk' to satisfy his hunger if a master would so honor him and how getting fucked was the way to gain sexual pleasure if your master would be so indulgent as to stick his prick up your ass when the mood struck him.

CHAPTER 15

Lunch

The executive dining room had been reserved just for Ramon and I and was beautifully furnished in native Brazilian woods throughout with the colorful fabrics all locally woven. But the meal itself was light and simple in keeping with the extreme heat outside. First course was a light salad with an iced fruit punch; second course was a braised chicken breast flavored with lime juice with brown rice served on the side; and the third course was Brazil nut ice cream topped with cream sauce. Two young male waiters, both absolutely superb specimens of masculine perfection, served the meal dressed in nothing more than jewel-incrusted gold slave collars, matching genital rings banded around their huge equipment for a prominent display, and gold rings through each tit. The two were matched by color, height, weight, body build, and genital size so they appeared to be brothers, if not twins. Both had beautiful curly brown hair allowed to grow below their ears, long thick brown eyelashes, green eyes, and ivory skin close-shaved from below their eyes to their ankles and coated with a fresh smelling oil of some type. Both gave impeccable service, maintained full erections throughout the entire time they were serving, and stood close enough between servings so that it was convenient to fondle them if you so desired. I was so impressed I asked my waiter if he had been bred on the farm here or if they had bought him somewhere.

The slave looked panicked when I addressed him and pointed to his lips.

"Slaves serving here in the executive suites are always muted," Ramon explained. "We don't want our confidential business talk being spread all over town by a bunch of gossipy slaves."

"Muted?" I asked. "You tear out their tongues?"

"Certainly not! We're not barbarians down here. Maybe in the States you do that, but not here," Ramon replied indigently. "It's a simple matter of cauterizing their vocal chords. Just takes a minute or so and other then the stench of burning flesh and some steam coming out of his throat and a few moment's pain, it's barely noticeable. It's all over in just a few minutes and they recover in no time at all. But its very effective. They won't say another word or anything resembling a word the rest of their life no matter what language they spoke. It's the best way to handle the confidentiality problem when you have slaves around. We call muting the oral shredding machine."

"Can they still swallow and breath all right and suck," I asked, rather naively.

"Of course, Bob. All we did was burn off their vocal chords - nothing else. It doesn't affect anything but speech. Ready for dessert?"

I nodded my assent. Ramon motioned to the waiters with an uplifted hand and instantly the ice cream was placed before me in a silver tulip cup. I couldn't see any sauce on it, however, but before I could comment, my waiters' throbbing penis was positioned directly over the ice cream with the waiter making a jerking motion with his right hand and looking at me quizzically.

"He wants to know if you want to serve your own sauce or you want him to serve," Ramon prompted.

I must have look totally confused, which I was, as I stared at the huge prick quivering in front of me and then Ramon.

"You want to pump him or you want him doing the pumping?" Ramon explained.

I told the slave to deliver the sauce and, without hesitation, he began jerking himself off directly aimed at the ice cream in front of me with a smile on his face. Ramon, always one to be in charge apparently, roughly grabbed his waiter's swollen shaft and began stoking it rapidly. The two slaves looked at each other and it was obvious they were in contest to see who could shoot their load first on their master's desserts. My waiter won by a second or so, but the volley of steaming hot cum produced by both slaves was prodigious. Both filled the silver serving bowls completely making sure they carefully coated the ice cream itself in the process. They were obviously pleased they had been allowed to relieve the long time pressure in their balls and thanked us with hand signs and huge smiles.

"They're never allowed to unload unless it's part and parcel of the meal - you know, saucing the meat, breakfast rolls, desserts, things like that. Sometimes they go for days without being allowed to empty those big balls of theirs. When the big moment comes, they're always very grateful to whatever master they're serving at that meal."

"Just the opposite of thanking a master for sucking a load down into their own bellies. It's obvious, training slaves involves teaching them to be versatile. But Ramon, this combination is delicious. Brazil nut ice cream with hot cum sauce - I'll have to remember that. It's the best sundae I've had in years. My favorite up until now was the mundane hot fudge sundae you can get at any Dairy Queen. You know, Ramon, I have a friend that owns a Dairy Queen in Philadelphia. If he offered this as an option, he'd drive everyone else out of business."

Ramon laughed at my joke heartedly, but then got somber. "Perhaps you should look into some new business ventures, Bob. There's a lot of money to be made using slaves effectively. You're still going to switch over to slave labor at your assembly plant, aren't you?"

"Yes, I answered, "if I can find what I need at the marketplace cheaply enough, Ramon."

"Oh, no problem with that if you buy up the middle-aged ugly ones. But, Bob, I was talking about some new ventures where the real money is."

"Like what, Ramon?"

"Ever thought about setting up a breeding operation outside of Philadelphia? From the sounds of it, the market is wide open there."

"Ramon, I don't have the capitol your family has available. Breeding slaves is terribly profitable, I know, but it's a long term investment. You have to buy up all those breeding wenches and a few good studs, feed and shelter them for at least 18 or 19 years before there is any payoff at all. I know you can work the wenches while they're in foal, but still, it's a long term investment and you have a lot of money tied up for years and years. Me, I'd have to borrow all that money and the interest would kill me before I could cash in. You, you've got your family resources so you don't need to worry about any interest charges, I'll wager."

"Point well taken, Bob. I didn't realize you were so poor, I guess. Don't you have any family that could help you out on such a sure win investment?"

"Ramon, I don't have any family at all. I was an only child whose parents died of cancer when I was barely 20, leaving me just enough to meet the interest payments on the assembly business I inherited."

"Well, some good friends then, Bob?" Ramon persisted.

"Ramon, you live in a totally different world of leisure and luxury and can't imagine how hard Americans have to work to make a buck. I have to work so hard to stay above water, I don't have time to make any friends, let alone keep one if I had one. It's taken three years of real sacrifice to even get enough to think about buying a bed buck for myself and the only reason that's necessary is because I don't even have a friend I know well enough to date, let alone bed down with. And those slaves I was planning on buying all have to bought on a bank loan. That's why the hotel I staying at with all that willing flesh around is just a dream come true for me. I think I have more of a social relationship with that Irish slave and that black slave I screwed there than I have with anyone back home. I guess you'd say I'm a real loner. That's why I really treasure our friendship and it means so much to me, Ramon."

"I wasn't exactly sure whether you had a family or good friends to look after your interests. Apparently none!" Ramon said with a strange, but excited look in his eyes." Well, poor and alone in the world as you are, apparently, I still want to bed you down, boy," Ramon giggled. "Maybe your poverty is your attraction."

I blushed at his comment, but not through shame. I was as sexually attracted to Ramon as he seemingly was with me and we did seem to get along quite well, despite his weird comments occasionally. We both finished our dessert, scooping the last drop of the delicious cum sauce out before departing as the slave waiting on us kneeled in respect with their eyes lowered, their knees carefully widespread to fully display their genitals, now semi-flaccid at last.

CHAPTER 16

The Shipping Department

As we got back to the rickshaw and its patient pony still sweating away in the torrid heat, Ramon asked if we should fuck the pony slave now.

"Right here in the street?" I asked.

"Why not? Everyone around here is used to seeing slaves being fucked most anywhere it's convenient," Ramon responded unemotionally. "The slaves don't care. Slaves can't afford modesty you know."

"For me, it's just too hot to enjoy it right here on the street, Ramon. I'll take a raincheck."

"In Brazil, it's never too hot to fuck, they say," Ramon laughed but quickly got into the rickshaw and grabbed the reins and whip so I jumped in beside him. "We'll go see the shipping department, although it's hot in there too to some degree. I think you'll be interested in seeing how slaves are caged for shipment all over the world, as well as prepared for their trip to the local markets."

It was another long ride, this time almost clear back to the main entrance of the farm.

"There are two main divisions: the international shipping division and the local division. I'll show you the international division first in that will show you how we ship slaves out to the States among other places. Then we'll see the local division which is mainly just preparing the slaves for final show at the marketplace and getting them herded into the delivery trucks. While we getting there," Ramon said as he whacked the whip a little more vigorously over the back of the gasping slave to hurry him along, "I'll explain the basics."

"For international shipping, we stop feeding the slave two days before shipment; then we give the slave a series of complete enemas to clean him out completely; then bath him completely so he starts out clean; and cuff his arms to his neck collar so he can't play with himself during shipment other than rubbing his prick against the bars of his cage. Then we catherize him , hooking him up to a collection jar beneath his cage, and coat his underarms and crotch with antiperspirant so he arrives sweet smelling. He can get water for the trip through a water nipple attached to the side of his cage, again hooked up to a supply jar attached to his cage. After that, it's just a matter of fork-lifting his cage onto a transport truck to take him to UPS airfreight facilities in Rio who get him on a plane within 5 hours at the maximum according to our priority shipment contract with them. He's in the States, whether its Chicago, New York, Miami, or whatever, within 8 to 10 hours and again receives priority unloading and reshipment on a UPS transport so he's in a local market there by the next day fresh and ready to be sold."

"The locals are even easier. All we have to do with them is cut off their food 48 hours ahead of shipment to cut down on the shit in them, give them a fresh body shave and purge their bowels out completely prior to shipment so they don't mess up the transfer truck or their holding cage once they are there and so their ass is clean to the touch when they're examined. They're chained together by the neck, but we leave both their feet and hands unshackled in that they need them to keep upright in the rough ride to the Rio markets. Then, with a good whip on their butts, they're loaded by groups of 20, all chained together, into the transport trucks which - you've probably seen them around town - are double decker with metal slats on the side for good ventilation but so they can see out and those on the streets can enjoy seeing them being taken to market. Each transport truck can handle 15 groups of 20 each if we really jam them in. That's better really in that they can't fall down that way - they just press against each other and so they don't get injured in shipment no matter how fast and crazy the driver takes them to market. About two hours to market - three in heavy traffic - and then they're unloaded into the holding cells there. They're given another bath and oiling before being shown and a few of them are up on the blocks and being sold by that night. The rest usually have found a new owner by the end of the next day if they're priced right."

By then, we were at the shipping department. Inside, it was exactly as Ramon had described except it didn't stink like I thought it would. The enema stations were very well ventilated with a constant flush of the floor beneath the slaves, the shaving stations only required the slave to stand absolutely still - almost guaranteed by the tight chaining by his neck collar. The antiperspirant they used smelled like fresh pine and was most appealing. The cages were so cramped no movement was possible no matter how small the slave: this allowed positioning him for easy installation of his catheter and made sure its connection to the tubing would stay in place as well as positioned the slave for easy access to the water nipple with his mouth. I imagined the flight would be painful due to the cramping, but it was only for 12 to 16 hours probably even if there were a few delays along the way. They probably couldn't walk for a few minutes after being uncaged, but after the blood got flowing again, they would be all right. Some slaves resisted a little being stuffed into the tiny cages and then being positioned for the catheter but each of the handlers carried a small electric prod on their belt to correct any resistance to either packing them in the cages or fixing a catheter down their cock. Some slaves looked excited; some looked resigned; some looked lethargic; some looked anxious; some were obviously high strung and nervous at this new development in their lives. But I saw no signs of resistance or rebellion. Apparently, all of that had been drummed out of them long ago in their training sessions. Most looked like they were ready to be sold - the training had produced the need to find an owner who would take care of them if they would just do everything he or she wanted - a good deal in their eyes now.

The local shipment division was a little more chaotic in that everything was done in groups - the docking as well as the body shaves and the only restraint was by their neck collars. This area too was fresh smelling despite the docking operations but the whips in constant motion and the sharp yelps from the slaves that were hit added a lot of noise to the scene. But it was loading the transport trucks where a lot of noise was concentrated. The whips seemed to be picking out each slave individually all over their bodies as each group was pushed and prodded into the crowded trucks. By the time the last groups were being forced in, there was so little room one handler spent all his time whipping the slaves already loaded to force them further back into the truck while another handler concentrated on whipping the slaves to be loaded to press themselves into the sea of vertical flesh on each deck of the huge trucks. Once loaded to full capacity, the tailgates were forced shut and the chorus of wails and moans from the trailers' inhabitants could be heard for blocks with the whips nipping at them through the grates. Hands were sticking out of every available opening on the sides of the trucks (the openings were too small for heads to fit through) and slaves got to screaming from the press of humanity all around them. Some were having trouble breathing so gasps and pants could be heard nearby as they struggled to get air by pressing against the outside grates; some were getting hard and even shooting off on each other from the excitement of having so many bodies rubbing against their sex; some were trying to jack off given this new freedom and lack of supervision despite the close quarters while those around them screamed their objections at being coated with the sticky white cum; others were trying to fuck their neighbor since the neighbor often couldn't move out of the way and could only scream his objections; and some, of course, got sick from the heat and lack of air and pure panic and started throwing up all over everyone else which led to another volley of curses and shouts from those feeling the warm vomit running down their bodies. I could see where the truck and its occupants would have to be hosed down immediately upon arriving and why full baths were scheduled for the slaves even before being put into holding cells, let alone before being shown to the public.

"Three hundred in each load," Ramon said proudly, oblivious to all the panic going on inside the trailers themselves. "People get a kick out of seeing them going down the streets toward the markets. They look especially like animals that way and clearly establishes just what slaves are in the public's eye. I guess that's why children seeing them like to jeer at the slaves and call them names. It's exciting to them, I suppose. But teenagers can be a problem in that they throw garbage at them and tease them about whose going to fuck them once they're sold. Usually something like 'you think you can take one as big as between my legs' or 'your new master is going to split you in two when he fucks you, whore.' Things like that which is so silly considering most of them couldn't afford the big finger of any one of those slaves, let alone their ass to fuck. What do you think of this part of the business, Bob?"

"Well organized, Ramon, but the sheer volume involved sort of overwhelms me. Just imagine how much capitol is jammed into one of these transport trucks. If it went over a cliff, it would be a financial disaster."

"Yes, the insurance costs are steep, all right, Bob. What's in one truck costs about the same as that little factory of yours, if it were paid for."

CHAPTER 17

My New Life

"That's a strange comparison, Ramon. How would you know the cost of my assembly plant?"

"Oh, I know most everything there is to know about you, Bob. That's why you will be staying here instead of going home with me tonight."

"Why, Ramon. Something wrong?"

"Quite the contrary, Bob. Those two handlers in back of you right now will be taking you to the newly enslaved training facilities just as soon as they can get the hand cuffs and neck collar on you," Ramon said calmly.

Sure enough, two huge muscular slaves swiftly moved behind me and instantaneously fitted a collar around my neck and, pulling my arms behind me, shackled them together by the wrist. Then, calmly, one of them took a pair of scissors and cut every stitch of clothing off of me until I was standing there right in the locking dock of the shipping center stark naked.

I sputtered with rage but found the neck collar so tight I could barely breathe, let alone talk.

"You see, Bob, we've researched your situation thoroughly. You have no family, no parents, no wife to get concerned about your absence. A simple press release will announce you disappeared on a recent trip to the Amazonian jungles hunting for wildlife and we have already bought up the mortgage on your assembly plant from the banks so we'll be taking possession on that shortly. All of your employees will be retained until the matter of your disappearance is accepted and then it will be converted to slave labor as you were planning to do anyway, except we find it a perfect destination for some fresh breeders who will be perfect workers at your plant even though the stud/supervisory slaves who will accompany them will make sure they work as hard as possible as well as be knocked up consistently. Your home, modest as it is, is also part of your plant mortgage, as you already know, so it becomes our property as well. It will be the nucleus of a new training facility for the Philadelphia market where we will train the new slave products from your plant as they become available and in the interim buy up promising American slaves to process for resale with some solid D'Salvantio training under their skin.

"As for yours truly, you're going to be a slave now for the rest of your life. But not just any slave, Bob. Once you've been thoroughly trained in the newly enslaved training program you just visited today, we're going to put you in stall #9 in the stud's holding cells right next to that other American stud from Alabama that was getting so lonely and to whom we promised some company soon. We're always good for our word, Bob, as you, of all people could appreciate. We said we'd take care of your problems and help you out and we certainly are - big time! Once our slaves at the hotel - yes, we own the hotel you were staying at as well as the travel agency you arranged your trip with - informed us of your physical qualifications for making a good stud as well as your insatiable sex drive (that studs always need if they're to be good at their job), it was just a matter of time until we found the right time to enslave you. We thought that videotaping you in action with those two slaves of mine back at the apartment so we could study the details of your sexual apparatus as well as your techniques, and then familiarizing you with a slave's life and reality through a complete visit to the farm here, it would be a lot easier to train you for what we have in mind. After all, you now know exactly what a stud here does and where he does it; where he sleeps and recharges; how slaves can be useful as ponies later in their life; how the bred products are trained as well as those, like yourself, newly enslaved; how slaves can be useful at waiting table as well as serving as milk studs, and finally, how all those pups you're going to produce for us are going to be shipped out to markets both internationally as well as locally. You'll be going into your slave training with some real advantages - a good general overview of the whole operation. It should help you accept your new life a lot easier... Bob... no... not Bob... 'slave' is the proper title now, isn't it?"

Before I could say one word, the slave handlers in back of me had jammed a huge penis gag down my throat and fastened it by straps around my head so I couldn't say a word but struggled to breathe and swallow. With a few quiet commands to the huge slaves holding me, he told them to take me to the newly enslaved training unit and make sure I was checked in and properly restrained on a saw horse where they could help out in the initial fucking exercises. Both slaves enthusiastically thanked their master for this rare opportunity and I could feel their erect pricks rubbing against my bare ass.

With that command, Ramon casually went back to the waiting rickshaw, ordered the slave to drop to his hands and knees with his ass open and then mounted the sweat drenched pony slave and fucked him as he watched the slave handlers drag me away.

I never saw him again until five months later when my slave training was complete and I was assigned to the stud unit. I no longer thought of myself as anything but a property of the D'Salvantio family maintained for the sole purpose of serving the family the very best way I could. Certainly, the D'Salvantio brand on my naked butt marked me as their property, but, more importantly, my every fiber told me my destiny was to be a slave for life. If that included baby-making for the breeding farm that owned me, then I intend to take pride in the quantity and quality of the slave pups I produce. If later I am assigned to pull a rickshaw, then I will pull it to be very best of my ability. And if my masters command me to offer them sexual pleasure, then I will offer all by body can produce.

Any memories of Philadelphia and cell phone component manufacture was all a distant and anxiety-ridden nightmare. Now I was secure, had a purpose in life, and contributed to the welfare of my master every way I could as was a slave's mission. I even had a good friend now - a new and novel experience for a lonely boy from Philadelphia - the very experienced stud slave named "Alabama" who had the holding cell right next to me and who loved his work on a breeding farm.

On my very first studding assignment, there my master Ramon was in the balcony surrounded by the usual bunch of Japanese tourists with their camera flashes going. When we waved to the observers as we had been taught before getting to the fucking assignment itself, I saw Ramon smile and wave back as he watched me get with my task and complete it to the best of my ability - exactly as I had been taught. When I was through, soaked in sweat and fully drained, I glanced up at him again with a prideful smile and was overjoyed when he gave me a 'thumbs up' sign of an owner's approval. For the first time in my life, I felt total satisfaction with my life and a feeling of peace, purposefulness, and contentment swept over me.

ABOUT THE AUTHOR

Bill Smith is a prolific writer of homoerotic novels which receive critical acclaim for their tightly constructed plots, their believable characters, and their writing craftsmanship. Three books already available from Nazca Plains are "Bates Training Center," "The Brazilian," and "Guiliano Imports."

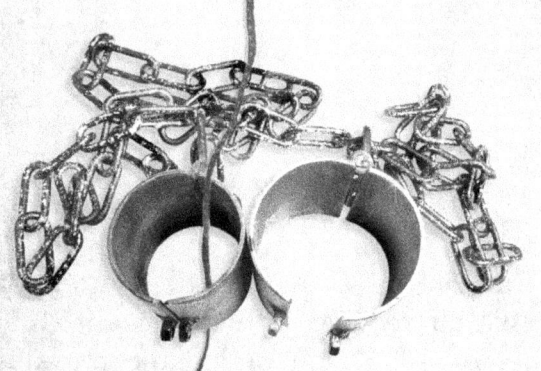

BATES
TRAINING CENTER

A NOVEL BY
BILL SMITH

A
RONER
BOOK

SMITH

BATES TRAINING CENTER

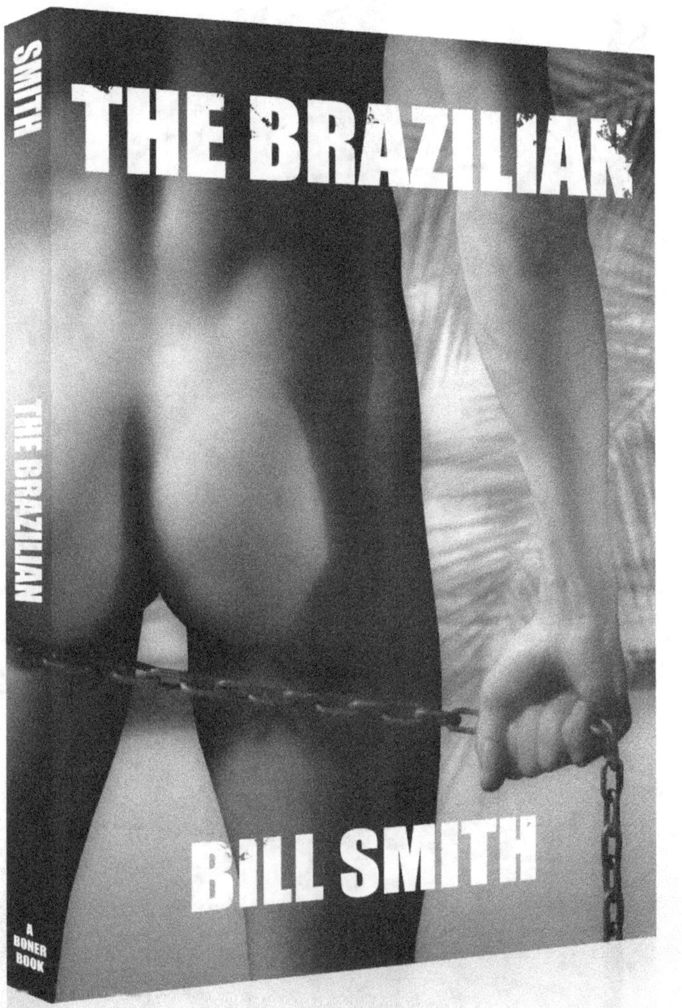
SMITH
THE BRAZILIAN
A BONER BOOK
THE BRAZILIAN
BILL SMITH

GUILIANO IMPORTS

A EROTIC TALE OF SATISFACTION GUARANTEED BY

BILL SMITH

A BONER BOOK

www.ingramcontent.com/pod-product-compliance
Lightning Source LLC
Chambersburg PA
CBHW051150260626
47170CB00005B/2048